Dunkirk

A World War II Novel

Richard G. Hole

Dunkirk
A World War II Novel

Richard G. Hole

World War II

1

SYNOPSIS

Leaning a little at the back of the trench, he watched the thick smoke drifting off the city of Dunkirk.

It was clear that merciless fighting was going on there, and that the men in the city must be having a pretty bad time.

Staring with wide blue eyes at the sergeant, the youngest of the platoon approached him.

There was a pleading tone in his voice when he said:

"Will we have time, Sergeant?

The sergeant did not turn, but asked:

"Time for what?

"To get there ...

Dunkirk is a story belonging to the World War II collection, a series of war novels developed in World War II.

DUNKIRK

CHAPTER I

Followed by his men, Adams jumped into the trench where an explosion had just occurred. He had perfectly seen the jump the French soldier made before he fell, when the mortar exploded not far from the unfortunate man. Now, as his boys occupied the little trench, Adams turned to the body and saw the huge cut shrapnel had made in the soldier's neck.

Ed Cooper sighed next to him.

"They have slaughtered him like a pig ..." he said.

Adams nodded. He kept looking at the man's body and, above all, the blood gushing from his neck. He only thought for a moment to help the Frenchman; but almost at once she must have shuddered from head to toe and her skin color changed, turning papery white.

Then he froze.

Sam, Horace, Peter, and Justin were at the other end of the trench, where the first two were setting up the machine gun. Ed was still at the sergeant's side, staring stupidly at the Frenchman's corpse. In the distance, to the left, the cannonade of the German tanks and the response that the French antitanks were making could be heard clearly.

"Shall we throw it out? Ed Cooper asked.

"Do not. Leave it there "replied the sergeant." I don't think we have to spend too long in this hole. It won't bother us anymore ...

A machine gun began firing violently in front of them. The bullets whistled over the heads of the English and they stuck to the bottom of the trench, letting the projectiles pass as if nothing had happened. Adams Shaw calmly sat down and lit a cigarette. A squad of Stukas passed, like heartbreaking thunder, overhead.

The dead man put a violent note in the trench. The bleeding had stopped and the wound was turning black. Some flies, hesitating at first, landed frankly on the face and advanced, with small leaps, towards the gap that had been made by the piece of shrapnel.

"Damn flies! Ed growled. They are the ones who take advantage ...

A mocking smile appeared on Adams Shaw's lips.

"They did not" he replied, looking at the soldier. It is the worms that will take advantage later. But what can that matter anymore?

Leaning a little at the back of the trench, he watched the thick smoke drifting off the city of Dunkirk. It was clear that merciless fighting was going on there, and that the men in the city must be having a pretty bad time.

Staring wide blue eyes at the sergeant, Justin Selby, the youngest of the platoon, approached him. There was a pleading tone in his voice when he said:

"Will we have time, Sergeant?

Adam did not turn around, but asked:

"Time for what?

"To get there.

"Are you not well here, little one?

"It's not that, sir," Selby replied. The boats are there, and therefore the only way to get home.

Then the sergeant did turn to him, staring at him.

"Why didn't you think better of it, Justin? You got carried away by the enthusiasm, right? It seems that I am seeing you, with the brand new uniform, saying goodbye to the boys of the neighborhood and looking at them, up and down, with contempt. You must have stayed home, boy. There was still a long time to go before you were called up. But you wanted to make yourself the hero ...

She realized that Justin's face was ashen. There was no clearer sign of fear and the sergeant recognized it at once, as if the boy had it painted on his face.

"Have a little patience" he said after a pause. We'll manage to get out of here.

"Thank my Lord.

"Go to your place now, boy.

"Yes.

They had strayed from the center of the German attack line. The entire company had taken on the job of guarding the right flank to prevent the Germans from carrying out one of their famous "bags," thus preventing many English and French from reaching the Dunkirk quay. It was natural for someone to dance with the ugliest, thought the sergeant. After all, as long as they were alive, they could tell.

Ed Cooper, who was at the front of the trench, turned at that moment.

" The tanks! He warned.

Looking away from Dunkirk, Adams Shaw went to his men and looked in the direction Cooper was pointing. Four brown spots advanced over the land.

Then he looked at the trench, satisfied that it was narrow and deep, like a ditch. It was the only defense they could afford against Nazi armor. Raising his voice, to control the boom of the first cannon shots that the tanks were already releasing, he shouted:

"You know what we have to do, guys! You have to let them pass over. Anti-tank guns are behind. What we have to prevent is the infantry from passing behind those pots.

Why had he repeated, once again, those instructions his men knew by heart? What had they done, for more than fourteen hours, other than shoot at German infantry clinging to carts, trying to penetrate the extreme neighborhoods of Dunkirk?

Smiled.

He was fed up with it all. And it was extremely painful to go back without rest, demonstrating to oneself the incapacity of the Army of which he was a part. He had arrived in France with the almost complete certainty that the Germans would meet, for the first time in that war, with the exact fit of his shoe. He even allowed some jokes, in England, when the events in Poland.

"The same will not happen to us," he had said. Those Poles are brave, no one doubts it, but they don't know how to wage war. You'll see when the Nazis will attack us ... »

But it had been a thousand times worse.

Adams had been in the Army for ten years, and it was extremely easy for him to read his true state of mind on the faces of his superiors. So when the Germans began to advance, he realized that this was going to be even a lot worse than what had happened in Poland. And when he was able to realize that fear was gripping everyone, that German superiority was prevailing everywhere, that disorganization was beginning to emerge in the English and French units, he felt a tremendous disgust.

But now he had no time to experience the same.

The tanks were approaching at full speed and his men crouched, nevertheless trying to see if the German infantry moved alongside the armor. With the machine gun that the platoon possessed, they had no illusions of stopping those steel monsters that spewed fire from all their cannons and machine guns. Nor was it possible to stop them with bombs, as some boys had tried, in Belgium, being crushed under the chains. They lacked much experience and none of them were prepared to fight the armor face to face. The earth began to tremble at the proximity of the heavy steel monsters.

But as soon as the tanks passed over them, the British leaned out again and placed the machine gun in position, firing at the German infantrymen who, protected by their armor, were trying to advance on that side. Weapons cracked relentlessly and Adams watched with satisfaction as the Germans threw themselves to the ground, some of them falling to keep up.

Almost at the same moment, the antitank guns that were located a hundred meters from the trench began to fire rapidly at the German armor. Some of the projectiles landed near the trench and produced a dry, horrid boom that left an intense pain in the ears.

After glancing at the place where the Germans had dropped to the ground and noting that they were not getting up, due to the intense fire from the machine gun, Adam Shaw turned and looked towards the German tanks, noting with satisfaction that two of them they were already burning and that another had just exploded, hit directly by a shell from the British guns.

He also observed that the occupants of one of the tanks jumped to the ground and fell back, running towards the trench, seeking the support of the German infantry. Then he raised the machine gun to his face and waited patiently for the Germans to come close. Then he squeezed the trigger and felt tremendous satisfaction at the leap the tank occupants made and the pirouettes they were doing before coming to a standstill on the ground.

How could he feel such satisfaction in killing?

He had gotten used to doing it too quickly. But perhaps that rage that seized him had been born when he saw the first corpses of his English companions and of his friends, the French.

It was a violent reaction to death, as if from the beginning he had stood somewhat apart and then suddenly entered the game of that curious lady who was, after all, the absolute owner of the battlefield.

Someone came from the left and Adams was about to shoot him. It was in a split second that he became aware of the uniform and the helmet, almost immediately recognizing Lieutenant Barney who, moments later, dropped into the trench.

He almost tripped over the body of the Frenchman and looked at him, then fixed his eyes on the sergeant's face.

"Who is it? " I ask.

Shaw shrugged.

"I don't know, sir. He almost died when we got here.

"Is everything going well in your platoon?

"Yes sir. You see ...

"Yes. The captain was just killed, sergeant. I have taken over the company. I bring orders from the battalion.

"Has the commander not reached Dunkirk?

"Yes, it has arrived there. And he has radioed with me. Two of the companies are already embarking. But we have to hold out a little longer.

"I understand.

"We will wait for the night to come," the officer continued. Then we will retreat. His platoon is the most advanced. Are there many Germans in front of you?

"A few, Lieutenant. But you can see that they have stayed still. They do not know how to do anything if they are not accompanied by a good handful of tanks.

The officer smiled.

"Things are not going very well at Dunkirk," he continued. Many die before reaching the ships and the launches leap into the air, torn apart by the Stukas' bombs. I don't know if we can get there, Sergeant ...

"We will do our best, sir.

Peter screamed at that moment.

"They come again!

The officer and the sergeant rushed to the side of the trench and watched as the German groups rose, advancing decisively towards them. Again the submachine gun barked and once again the Germans had to stick to the ground. But there was no doubt that this situation could not last too long.

Lieutenant Barney sighed.

Then he said:

"Try to hold out as long as you can, Shaw. It is necessary that the Germans do not penetrate from this side. It would be catastrophic for those trying to board. On the other hand "he explained" the French are resisting quite well and have allowed two regiments to embark, almost whole. We have to do our part.

"Of course.

The lieutenant looked at the Germans once more, quickly calculating their numbers and concluding that Shaw's platoon machine gun could stop them, still for some time. Then, putting his hand on the sleeve of the sergeant's torn jacket, he said:

"I'm going back to the company, sergeant. And remember that at dusk you have to leave the trench.

"Yes Sir!

The German fire had subsided somewhat and Lieutenant Barney, taking advantage of the moment, jumped quickly from the trench.

He never should have.

He had barely brought his knees to the rear edge of the parapet when he spun and fell flat on his face, shuddering from head to toe. The sergeant ran up to him and so did Justin Selby. They both yanked on the lieutenant's feet and then caught him, laying him carefully at the bottom of the trench.

Young Justin felt a chill run down his spine.

As unlikely as it seemed, Barney had received two bullets: one in the left shoulder, which had made him spin quickly, and another, the ugliest-looking one, right in the mouth. Blood flowed profusely from the second of the wounds, and the officer's eyes were wide with an expression of unspeakable horror. He looked at the sergeant and then his hand, which had passed over his face and had withdrawn soaked in blood, moved to the right breast pocket of the warrior, trying to undo it.

Adams rushed to help him.

He took out his briefcase and it was enough to look into the lieutenant's eyes to understand what he wanted. The poor officer must have suffered horribly, and now an abundant foam was mixing with the blood that came from the place where his mouth had been almost completely torn off by the projectile.

Breathing difficulties appeared almost immediately and death rushed forward, by leaps and bounds as the officer's body suffered from constant convulsions and ended up stiffening, becoming stiff as a stick, clenching his fists until his knuckles turned completely white.

Justin covered his eyes in horror.

"My God! He exclaimed.

Biting his lip, Adams slightly opened his wallet and looked at the photographs he already knew. Barney's wife and two children: Two beautiful little boys, twins, about eight years old, laughing at the door of their house, next to their mother, a very pretty woman with long golden hair.

Stuffing the lieutenant's documentation in his pocket, Adams turned to look at the Germans who were still receiving the bullets from the submachine gun. He then observed that the Germans began to withdraw, in groups. He did not want to say aloud the enormities he was thinking and fired a burst with his submachine gun, wishing that the bullets would tear off the opponent's pieces of meat so that he would pay, with the highest price, what he had just done in the person of the Lieutenant Barney.

Beside him, in a whimpering voice, Justin Selby said:

"We must go, sir... We won't have time to do it later.

She turned to him, glaring at him with the fierceness of her gaze.

"Hush, you idiot! He roared. You think only of your miserable skin

...

The soldier walked away, scared.

Glancing back at the lieutenant, Adams Shaw released a string of curses to finish telling himself that it was very likely that they, all, ended up in the same or similar way.

The roar of combat did not cease throughout the afternoon.

But the Germans did not appear again before the trench occupied by Shaw's platoon and Shaw, like his men, remained attentive during those endless hours, observing from afar, with curiosity not without anguish, the uninterrupted attacks of the German aviation that did not cease to fly over, not a single moment, the dense cloud that marked the place where Dunkirk was.

Adams perfectly understood the mood of his men.

They were looking forward to the night to leave that place and make their way, whatever it was, to the port where the only possible salvation awaited them. But the funny thing is that he did not experience the same, far from it. I sincerely wish that things had completely turned around and that the Allied Armies found themselves with enough power to show the adversary that they were not going to flee like rabbits, but that they would attack once more, expanding the beachhead in which now They were moving around and getting the Nazis back, teaching them a lesson they could never forget.

You are deluded, Adams, he told himself, with infinite bitterness. Your duty is to take these men to the port and bring them back to England. Stop the nonsense. They cannot experience the same as you. How do you want them to know your bitterness? It would have been much better if this Frenchman or Lieutenant Barney were still alive and that those bullets that ended their stock were stuck in your body. But is it possible that you wish for death this way? Does that bitch deserve it ...? »

How easy it was to get carried away by memories in those moments!

Although no one was to blame that he had been a perfect idiot. And it wasn't that they hadn't noticed. Everyone, his family, his friends ... They had told him a thousand times, carefully, knowing that he was not going to consent, in any way, that someone allowed himself the luxury of speaking ill of that woman with whom he was madly in love.

How blind he had been!

There was no greater truth in life than that which said that the deceived man is the last to realize the deceit of which he is the object. But the truth, much more true than everything, was all the emotion he experienced when he was close to her, when he could look into her eyes, when her hands were intertwined with hers, when he felt the contact of Deborah's morbid flesh, when the sweet and warm taste of her lips remained on his mouth ...

Remember...

It was as if the bandages that covered their wounds were removed from a sick person, as if the strips of tape were suddenly ripped off and pieces of skin were taken away, without scruples and without mercy. But that, oddly enough, pleased him. Little by little he had gotten used to hurting himself, picking at that ulcer, with real passion.

It was as if he wanted to pay, indefinitely, the price of a betrayal he had been the last to know. And now, when the faces of his close friends paraded before him, with that ironic smile that they dared to put on their lips later, when he learned the truth, he felt his body stiffen, his muscles knotting under his skin and a gnashing of teeth was produced in his mouth that was filled with a bitter taste, like of bile ...

And worst of all is that he had not listened to the advice, that he had covered his ears and closed his eyes to the words and images that so many tried to awaken in his dormant brain, dominated by passion. And when he had the courage to take her to the mayor's office, when he made the dreadful mistake of giving her his name, he felt, the very fool, so completely happy and blissful that now he was stirring with rage, as if those moments had been the worst of his life. life.

Why hadn't he killed her? Why did he leave the terrible affront unpunished?

It seemed a lie to her that he could have behaved in that stupid way and that instead of reproaching him for everything he did to her, before and after getting married, he brutally abandoned her, but without saying a single word, leaving her at the house that had cost him so much effort. riding and, what was even worse, giving her the possibility, which was now more obvious than ever, to become a war widow, with a beautiful pension that could be spent on all the oils, which she did not really need, but which increased to the indescribable the wild beauty of his face.

How she had struggled with bitterness and how she had hidden from everyone the hideous problem within her!

Because nobody knew a single word. At least in the unit where he fought. Even the very stupid man kept writing letters, the answer to which never came. Letters showing others that he was a happy man, that he had not been the poor jester, in the hands of that woman, who had recognized in him, from the first time they met, the easy, docile and simple instrument of his intolerable coquetry.

He would have gladly ripped the skin off his hands when he remembered the caresses he gave to a spurious flesh, over which other hands, countless hands, had passed before him. He would have cut his lips with a knife, mercilessly to his own pain, thinking of the kisses he put on the mouth that other lips had kissed many times and that were capable of simulating a passion and an innocence much worse than the deception that committed.

He wondered if it was possible that all this produced in him a kind of almost complete abandonment to his own safety. It made him angry to imagine that the bravery he had shown from the beginning of the war was the daughter of his own despair. Because she had tried, in a thousand different ways, to remove that part of her past from him, to rip it out of her heart and her brain, without succeeding.

The self-contempt he felt was of no use to him, the urgent need to get it over with once and for all and to forget, in the broadest sense of the word, when death came to him. They had been futile efforts, wasted. And now, remembering his misfortune once more, he once again pleased himself by hurting himself as much as possible, tearing himself inside with relish, torturing himself in such a way that he shuddered, from head to toe, as if he were already dying with the convulsions he had seen. , shortly before, in the body of the lieutenant, shuddering in agony before dying.

He reached into his pocket where he had put Barney's papers and the photograph he knew so well. He didn't dare to pull out his wallet, however. But he thought that the death of a man can matter little when he leaves something positive and well built in life. It was easy to imagine that the officer's last thoughts had flown over the lands and waters, to be projected, with a force full of affection, on those people who reproduced the photograph taken at the door of the small house, in a popular London neighborhood. . Yes, there was no doubt that there is a kind of justification, even in the face of death, when you leave behind a deep and sincere trace of something as positive as people who will mourn you, who will remember you fondly ...

But he was like an abandoned dog. A despicable being, whom everyone laughed at, a kind of comic caricature that he had drawn, with his obscene gestures, the dirty hand of a woman whom he passionately kissed many times ...

CHAPTER II

Justin Selby walked over to him.

"It's already night, sir ..." he said, in a low voice. Adams Shaw nodded.

"Yes, boy. You are right. We will have to start leaving here.

It was almost completely dark, as the city fires and the bomb explosions, which continued to explode behind them, cast a reddish light on the horizon, as if a death sunset were inscribed on the earth and sky.

The sergeant approached his men.

"Let's get ready, guys" he said. We will go out with great care. I have not the slightest idea of the path to follow. But the fires will guide us. Hopefully we get a bit of luck and get to the port before the last ship has left.

He gave specific instructions for the platoon to open up and put Selby and Fells in the rear, letting Sam, Horace, and Ed go in the middle and taking himself, the machine gun tightly in his hands, in the lead.

They left the trench.

They did not even think of burying the dead.

"For what?

Better for the Germans to do it when it was all over. Then, Shaw thought, they would seize the corpses by their feet and throw them into the trenches, then covering them at full speed, satisfied with what they had done, glad that they had obtained this resounding triumph over the English and Gallic forces.

They advanced as quickly as possible, stumbling over other trenches and other immobile bodies. Hundreds of dead that covered the ground everywhere, men who had thought, like them, of the beautiful possibility of escaping from that gigantic stocks and of being able to return to England, if only to start over again, preparing to continue the fight against the black power that had arisen in Berlin.

In the light of the fires, the Stukas continued to wail their sirens and drop their bombs, in the impressive dive flights, then making the air crackle, with horrid sound and projecting the high foam of the water up high, accompanied by the pieces of the boats that were hit by the bombs.

But the sergeant and his men were still too far from Dunkirk to realize the dire reality of this hell. They were moving through a dark area, in the midst of a maximum stillness, which was far more impressive than the roar of the explosions at Dunkirk.

Death had become the absolute owner of that land and seemed to smile, crouched, waiting for the opportunity to continue reaping life after life, with a truly inconceivable longing.

Shaw had managed to put the sad thoughts that had tortured him out of his mind and now he became the man of always, the leader of his platoon, aware of everything around him, ready to pull the trigger and get rid of everyone. how many enemies showed up. But neither he nor his men could escape the strange tranquility that surrounded them. It was as if they had suddenly ended up in a strange, paradoxical world, too silent and black to be true. Justin, who was next to Peter, in the rear of the platoon, his teeth were chattering and he made tremendous efforts so that the noise was not perceived by his partner, who was walking beside him.

He thought of his parents, in his house, in the garden where he used to work on Sunday mornings, arranging the flowers that his mother loved so much. He already imagined the joy of the woman and the strong hug she would give him when he arrived at her side and then, also, in the long and chilling story that she would do in front of her friends, in the corner bar, next to the square. A childish desire for heroism had possessed him from the beginning.

He was ready to prevent, whatever it was, that someone noticed and discovered in the depths of his soul the fear that overwhelmed him from the first fight. Right now he was shaking from head to toe, and yet he let himself be swept away by the smiling images of the near future.

Despite the optimism that was sandwiched between the fear, which he continued to experience, what Justin Selby could not forget was the image of the lieutenant, and the memory of that death gave him chills. He had not, at any time, fully assimilated what death represented in war. Even when he saw the first corpses, back in Belgium, before the great retreat, he wondered if he was not attending a film section and if those bodies, which fell around him, were not going to get up moments later when the director of the scene ordered to stop work.

It was as if his childhood imagination was helping him, in a way, to defend himself against the horror that around him wanted to influence him in a more terrible and direct way. But abandoning all those ideas, he focused his mind on what would happen when he got home and that managed to reassure him enough, even bringing a poor smile of hope to his tremulous lips.

He admired in his companions the apparent indifference they possessed. Of course they were all grown men and lacked imagination at all. He glanced at the man walking beside him and was overcome with envy, telling himself that he would give anything to look like the quiet Peter Fells.

Peter was a former miner from the southern part of England, and life didn't usually get too complicated. The same happened to the others, to Sam Blue, to Horace Colton ... and a little to Ed Cooper, although this one was quite different from the others. Sergeant Shaw used to call Cooper "the idealist."

A former student, he used to encourage his classmates with real speeches, explaining the secret reasons for that war and also showing them his deep knowledge of international politics. Thanks to him, his platoon mates learned about the birth of Nazism, the chaotic situation in postwar Germany, as well as the circumstances that had favored

Adolf Hitler, providing him with the unique opportunity in history to reach, at dizzying speed, up to the power.

As a student, Ed Cooper admired the German scientists and used to say that if they had achieved power, in the style of those old Greek republics, in which the sages were, at the same time, the rulers, a different destiny would have taken. Germany. Adams Shaw was the only one who used to laugh in Cooper's face, calling him delusional and other things.

But Justin Selby, like the rest of the squad, admired this tall, lanky boy with curly blond hair and deep blue eyes. Thanks to Cooper, they had had a long time of fun, listening to his easy verb, his word always fair and wise. They also loved the clear vision that Ed had of things and, above all, the enthusiasm that he put into all his talks.

At that moment, Adams stopped and gestured for his men to follow suit.

Going forward, Sam Blue, holding the submachine gun, asked in a low voice:

"Is something wrong, sir?

"I don't know," replied the sergeant. I heard a noise on the left ...

Blue looked that way, trying to perceive something in the darkness that, on this side, was more intense than on the right, where the fires of the city illuminated the path quite well. But he could see absolutely nothing, although he remained motionless, waiting for the sergeant to order the march.

Indeed, Shaw, after a few seconds of waiting, muttered:

"I must have been wrong. Go...

And it was at that precise moment that, suddenly, a blinding light enveloped them. Two reflectors, crossing each other, had caught them between their luminous rays, immobilizing them completely, making them see the impossibility of fleeing, since they had become perfect targets for the Germans who must have been close to the reflectors, with the index on the trigger. .

A hoarse voice, too hoarse to speak English, giving that tongue an oddly guttural sound, called out:

"Drop your weapons! You are surrounded!

For a few tenths of a second, Adams Shaw calculated their chances of escaping. They were null, completely non-existent. Resisting would have been insane and Shaw understood right away. Therefore, knowing that his men would not do anything until he ordered it, he was the first to throw the submachine gun, angrily, at his feet, while shouting:

"Obey!

Beside him, Sam Blue dropped the submachine gun and so did Horace, Ed, Peter, and Justin with their respective rifles. The hoarse voice rang out again:

"Hands behind your neck, quick!

They obeyed.

Then, in the luminous zone, half a dozen German soldiers appeared, pointing their rifles at them, approached them. A little to the left, a Nazi officer, pistol in hand, did the same. Seconds later they were surrounded and the officer, who was the one who had yelled at them, said, approaching the sergeant:

"You guys were lucky, dogs. We should have killed you …

Adams stared at the German.

"Why do not you do it? He inquired, with a sure and firm voice.

The officer went to make a gesture, but one of the soldiers, who was closer to him than Shaw, stepped forward. The rifle made a rapid circle and the butt struck on the right side of Shaw's face, and he was projected backwards as he felt a kind of stinging sensation on his face. He fell backwards, remaining on the ground, with the palms of his hands resting on the ground.

The officer spoke to the soldier in German and the soldier smiled. Then, approaching the British sergeant, the German said:

"You have to start learning, friend. Your tongue is too long. Standing!

Adams sat up, then running his hand over his cheek and feeling the contact with the blood gushing from the wound. He didn't say anything, just biting his lip. Meanwhile, a couple of German soldiers were searching the British and then it was his turn, feeling with distaste the hands of those men who searched his pockets and took away everything he had on him, including Lieutenant Barney's documentation. . But he could not resist and said, addressing the officer:

"It is the portfolio of the lieutenant who died recently. He entrusted it to me to send to his family.

The German smiled.

"We will send it to you", he replied. We will deliver it to your wife, in your own hand. Because very soon we will be in your disgusting country.

Shaw didn't say anything.

Forcing them to put their hands behind their heads, they were pushed back, taking a path that progressively away from Dunkirk. Justin Selby, between Ed Cooper and Peter Fells, let tears run down his youthful cheeks. More than scared he was desperate to see that it was very likely that he would never return to England. He was infinitely miserable and crying, deep down, was doing him a bit of good.

They walked all night.

Now they were marching down a road, walking along the ditch so as not to disturb the German armored vehicles and trucks that, incalculable numbers, were moving south. The occupants of those vehicles paid little attention to them and just looked at them, their faces serious and somber. The officer and his men walked alongside them, but only two of the German soldiers had their rifles in their hands and the others had put him on their shoulders, completely convinced that the English were not going to make any attempt to escape.

Later they were made to stop and get into some trucks, handing them over to new soldiers, under the command of a sergeant who greeted the officer militarily, standing before him.

Adams Shaw couldn't understand a single word of what these men were talking about and he saw them smile, smoke quietly while they still forced their hands to the back of their necks, a position that produced cramps in their arms.

The sergeant had not yet assimilated his new situation and he was stunned, unable to measure the reality of what was happening to him. He looked at his men and noted with satisfaction that they were all calm; I mean, all of them except Justin Selby who kept crying.

For the first time, he felt sorry for the young man and told himself that it had been a real bad luck for him to have signed up early.

But there was no longer a remedy.

Four German soldiers got into the truck, along with the prisoners, and the vehicle immediately started up. Throughout the night, without stopping, the truck headed north, on increasingly quieter roads, the agglomeration of troops succeeding a series of guard posts and later joining other trucks loaded with prisoners who were still in the same direction.

When it was dawn, one of the German soldiers indicated that they could sit down and the prisoners obeyed, lowering their hands.

Sam Blue then showed his audacity by begging the Germans for a cigarette.

"They took everything from us," he explained, smiling. And I really want to smoke …

The soldier smiled and took out a pack of cigarettes, handing them out to the prisoners. He was a man in his thirties, with a characteristic peasant face and apparently endowed with a large heart. Then he invited them to have a drink from his own canteen and the incorrigible Blue, after tasting the liquid, said:

"This is French brandy, right, Sergeant?

"I think so," Shaw replied.

"It is seen that they do not forgive anything" continued Sam. They are like lobster ...

Ed Cooper smiled.

"The wars have made no progress in that regard," he said, with that doctoral tone that made Adams Shaw smile. The victor takes what he wants from the land of the defeated. But this is one of the reasons that makes them most obnoxious.

"Aren't you going to drop us another of your scrolls? Fells inquired.

"Don't be afraid," Cooper replied. Have you already thought about what awaits us?

It was Justin Selby, wide-eyed, who asked, in turn:

"What do you mean, Ed?

"That the bad times haven't started yet, boy" Cooper replied. I hope they don't send us to a concentration camp where we are mixed with political detainees and Jews. It would be terrible! I have read too many things on that subject ...

No one noticed the shudder that shook Fells's body.

Because he was Jewish.

The trucks continued on their way, then veered clearly to the east. They had entered Germany and ran all day, stopping only a little, in a very clean town, where the soldiers ate and an infamous ranch was distributed to the prisoners. Anyway, Adams and his men devoured it with real appetite and would have repeated if the magnanimity of the Germans had made it possible.

Later, when the trucks started moving again, Justin Selby did his best to sit next to the sergeant.

"Sir ..." he said.

Shaw looked at him.

"What do you want, little one? He inquired.

"I wanted to speak to you, my sergeant.

"Speaks.

"You see ..." Justin hesitated. I was thinking that I could ask the Germans to send me home.

"You've gone mad?

"It is not that, sir. I can show you that I am not of the age to be a soldier. They have no right to lock me up in a concentration camp.

Adams Shaw smiled.

"Have a little patience, friend" he said. Things are not going to be as dire as they seem. In addition, we will organize ourselves to live the best possible life. You have to face the bad times, Justin.

"You are right, sir," replied the boy.

But he had his idea. And he glanced at Peter Fells, wondering if it was worth risking everything for everything. He was not willing, in any way, to endure the long confinement in a concentration camp. For even though he was hardly more than a child, he fully understood that the Allies were going to lose the war and that it would therefore be months, perhaps years, before he could return to England, if ever. such a thing possible.

Unable to realize, on the other hand, the terrible reality that was coming, Justin Selby voluntarily let himself be carried away by his own project, which he had imagined shortly before, when he remembered a phrase from Fells and associated it with what Ed Cooper had explained moments before.

The consequences of what he was about to do mattered little to him, since he was almost completely certain that he was going to be favored after all.

Meanwhile, as dusk began to dawn, the trucks continued on their way and they all stopped, when the dark night completely enveloped the caravan. They were made to get out of the cars and formed, in a long line, English and French, then made them advance towards the gigantic gate of the concentration camp to which they had been assigned.

The look of it all, bleak and gloomy, so impressed Justin Selby that he was on the point of crying again.

High barbed wire formed an impressive barrier and you could see the observation towers, where the Germans, with searchlights and machine guns, closely watched the prisoners. The first part they traversed looked quite normal, but as they passed the second row of barbed wire, plunging straight into the field, the appearance of everything around them changed like a charm.

The barracks, located on either side of the central promenade, were almost entirely destroyed by rain, sun, and wind. Its roofs, formed by a simple tarred fabric, offered a multitude of holes and its interior was not different from the sad appearance they offered on the outside. Piles of smelly straw marked where the prisoners slept, and a strong stench of humanity wafted everywhere.

They were assigned a corner where they dropped, silently, gazing at the others who had been captured before them and who were also looking at them curiously. A single bulb, covered in black fly droppings, dimly illuminated the interior of the barrack. One had only to look closely at the faces of those who were already there to understand that calamities were the absolute masters of life in the countryside.

The uniforms were ruined and the faces pale, haggard, with bright pupils and almost white lips. Sitting in his corner, Justin Selby told himself that he would not stay there long and that he was going to be, luckily, one of the lucky ones who would get away from that hell very soon, escaping the despair that he could read, clearly, in the face of his captive companions, in the dull stares and haggard faces that surrounded him.

Of course I would do things carefully, without anyone knowing.

But he didn't even care that he couldn't say goodbye to his friends, to his squad mates. They would lead him elsewhere and it was even possible, if Germany succeeded in invading Great Britain, that he might soon return home, even if the streets of English cities were full of successful Nazi soldiers.

What could that matter to him?

CHAPTER III

Heinrich Slassen laughed contentedly.

The order by which he had been appointed, that very morning, head of Stalag XXIII, in the absence of Major Drunker, who had joined the front, filled him with joy. It was obvious that this meant some kind of promotion, if not in category gallons, since it gave him omnimous power over about two thousand prisoners. Of course, all this was due to his direct participation, since 1933, in the political life of the National Socialist Party.

He was very lucky to pass at the opportune moment, changing his body, leaving the SA to become an integral part of the SS. He still welcomed the clear perception he had had, especially when rumors of the plot that had been he was preparing within the SA, destined to break the impetus of Adolf Hitler and put in his place the ambitious Rohm who, undoubtedly, had believed that the moment of his exaltation to power had arrived.

Seated in his office as chief of the Stalag XXIII, Oberleutnant Heinrich Slassen now recalled, with real relish, his early days which corresponded to the babbling of National Socialism in Germany.

The SA (Sturmabteilung, Assault Sections) were inextricably linked, in its creation, to the person of Göering who was its superior head in December 1922. In November 1925, the SS (Socialdemokratische Partei Deutschlands, German Social Democratic Party) were created.) and, from then on, a dark and secret fight began between the two organizations. In January 1931, Rohm took over the leadership of the SA General Staff, and thereafter he began to conceive serious hopes that were aimed at making him the new Führer of the nation of Germany.

But Rohm forgot that Hitler was constantly being informed of the ambitions and movements of those around him. And so, on the dreadful night of June 30, 1934, the Führer, accompanied by his trusted men, proceeded to the general cleaning within the SA It was the Obergfiruppenführer of the SA Lutze, Pfeffer's former assistant, who denounced Rohm's ambitions, speaking of them to Von Reichenau. Before all those murmurs reached Adolf Hitler's ears, Rover, the Gauleiter of Oldenburg, proposed the immediate arrest of the ambitious Rohm, on the grounds that if he came within his jurisdiction, he could attack him based on article 175 of the Code Criminal, referring to homosexuality.

Meanwhile, the news was reaching the Führer who realized that it was quite possible, indeed, that Rohm was preparing a "putsch."

At five in the morning of that sad day, a long line of cars, protected by a Reishswehr armored car, approached Wiessee where Rohm, completely calm, slept in the famous Hanslbaver pension.

Hitler was accompanied by a group of former personal guards, with whom he used to go to all political meetings. Also with him were Emil Maurice and the former horse dealer, Christian Weber. When they arrived at the boarding house, they were greeted by Count Von Spreti, whom Hitler struck in the face with the pommel of the ancient riding crop that he was so pleased to carry with him.

Immediately afterwards, Rohm was detained in his room, having to be awakened, as he was sleeping soundly.

Rohm was handcuffed and taken to Munich as a prisoner of state.

Meanwhile, Hermann Göering, equipped with means of combat and using armored vehicles, had surrounded the main house of the SA, seizing all the war material, weapons and ammunition and taking all its occupants prisoner.

Approximately two hundred heads of the SA were locked up in Munich, in the Stadelheim prison. Rohm was surprised by that arrest and did nothing but protest, to those who visited him, that he had always fought alongside Hitler and that the idea of rebelling against the Führer never crossed his mind.

Meanwhile, in the Brown House, Hitler studied the list of detainees and marked, underlining them with a red pencil, one hundred and ten of them. They were the men who should die. But the arrival of Franz, the Bavarian Minister of Justice, caused Adolf Hitler to finally reduce that list to nineteen names. At the head, of course, was Rohm, whom the Führer had a pistol brought to his cell, hoping it would end his life. But Rohm refused to commit suicide and, along with his companions, was shot in the courtyard of the Stadelheim prison in Munich in the early morning of June 1.

Two months earlier, the cunning Heinrich Slassen had voluntarily gone over to the SS

And now he was glad he did, having taken that precaution.

Remembering that horrible night, he shuddered. He could have been at the SA house in Berlin, being one of the detainees of the mighty Hermann Göering, when he showed up with his armored cars, surrounding the building. But luck had once again favored him, and now he could congratulate himself for having "sniffed" that situation that could have been definitely tragic for him.

He raised his head when he heard a knock on the door.

" Go ahead! He exclaimed.

Moments later, his henchman, Feldwebel Dietrich Klossen, stood before his superior.

"New prisoners have arrived, Lieutenant" said the sergeant.

"Many?

"Two hundred and eighty-three, exactly.

"Have they been housed already?

"Yes. On islet 16. There are 112 Englishmen among them. The rest are French.

"Agree. We are awaiting orders from Berlin. You know, Klossen, that I have proposed to employ these prisoners in the nearby armament factories. There are missions that they can easily carry out, thus earning food that we would otherwise have to give them as gifts. Herr Funker, the owner of one of these factories, has told me about the difficulties that currently exist in the casting room. And it would be a real shame if good German workers, of the Aryan race, became lung-sick while all these bums and pigs bask in the fields, killing each other their lice, don't you think?

"It is a magnificent idea, sir.

"Tomorrow we will go to see Herr Funker, although we have not yet received instructions from Berlin. I hope they don't take long to send them to us.

"As you wish, Lieutenant.

"Is there something else?

"No, nothing. I will distribute the ranch of the night to the newcomers. Although it is a can ...

"Why?

"Because we've already turned off the kitchens, sir. We did not expect the arrival of these men at this time.

"What a problem! Don't bother the cooks, Dietrich. No need to distribute food tonight. Let those pigs sleep and then tomorrow morning they'll have more of an appetite.

The Feldwebel steadied himself, then raised his right arm.

"Heil Hitler!

"Heil! The Oberleutnant merely replied.

The sirens began to roar before the day was born.

Shaking off sleep and fatigue, the prisoners left the barracks and formed the long walk, in that sinister barrier, which divided the camp into two equal parts. The light from the searchlights broadly illuminated the entire sector and shortly after the German soldiers in charge of the formation arrived. They were armed with a pistol, which they almost never drew and, on the contrary, carried a rubber baton in their hand with which they beat the retarded.

Despite the time of year, the cold was intense in that region, and the fatigue of the previous day could be seen on the faces of those who had arrived with Adams Shaw and the men in his platoon.

Shortly afterwards the head of the camp appeared, impeccably dressed. He reviewed the prisoners and then, standing roughly in the middle of the street, at whose sides the men were lined up, he said, speaking in German and interrupting from time to time so that the interpreter, who was next to him, could translate, first in English and then in French, his words.

"I am not fond of speeches" he began to say. Nor do I like to remind you that you are prisoners, because you can see that. What I do want to tell you is that you are going to have the possibility of living in a dignified way, earning your food and how many things Germany will give you generously. It is almost certain that some of you, if not many, are thinking that there are agreements, signed in Geneva, which prevent the use of prisoners of war. We, the National Socialists, are willing and we want, above all, that the men who are preparing to work do so voluntarily. No one will be forced to go to the factories, but, of course, those who accept this job will enjoy a life, food and care that we cannot provide for others. And since I like to know what kind of people have fallen to my luck, I want those who wish to work for the German War Industry to step forward the moment the whistle blows. Understood?

The interpreter blew the whistle moments later.

There was a moment of anticipation, and then suddenly, to general amazement, only one man stood out from the ranks of the prisoners.

Justin Selby.

Standing by the sergeant's side, even Adams Shaw gestured to stop the young man. But it was too late and Selby had taken the fatal step forward.

Almost immediately, a dull murmur spread through the ranks of the prisoners and the violent lash of some insulting words was heard in French and English.

"Pork!

"Pig!

"Traitor!

"Outdated!

Oberleutnant Henrich Slassen roared with rage.

"Hush, you sons of bitches!

His face was decomposed, but a wry smile touched his lips as he approached, with measured steps, towards the only volunteer, before whom he stopped.

"Very good guy. You see how your colleagues treat you. But don't worry, are you willing to work for Germany?

Justin Selby had turned intensely red and it took him a lot to say:

"Yes sir. Besides, I needed to speak to you, in private.

The smile deepened on the German's lips.

"Perfect. Come with me". He turned to the Feldwebel, saying in German, "Send those pigs to their barracks! Let there be no distribution of ranch until further notice!

Dietrich Klossen clicked his heels, then turned to the interpreter to have him translate the officer's orders.

Framed by the soldiers accompanying the German lieutenant, Justin Selby left the camp and was ushered into Slassen's own office, who showed him a chair.

"Sit down, friend" he said. Then he opened his gold cigarette case and offered him a cigarette which the young man admitted, flushing once more.

Heinrich looked at him curiously:

"I was very satisfied," he explained, "that you were the only volunteer. You will win, boy. But, it seems to me that you said you wanted to talk to me in private. It is not like this?

"Yes, sir," said the Englishman, surprised that Slassen didn't need an interpreter then. In fact, Heinrich spoke English quite well, but he believed that it would lose importance if he addressed the prisoners directly, preferring in any case to use the interpreter.

"What is it about?

Justin Selby hesitated.

The insults directed at him by the prisoners were still ringing in his ears. Was he doing well?

Hadn't he suddenly become a dirty traitor?

He undone those ideas, convinced that he was working for his own good, since none of those who had remained in the field would have raised a single finger to help him in his purposes. Raising his head, he looked calmly at the German.

"This is something important, sir.

"Speaks.

"There is a Jew in my platoon.

The smile that then appeared on Slassen's lips was full of cruelty.

" Very interesting! Are you sure, at least?

"Completely, sir.

"What is the name of that man?

"Peter Fells, sir.

" Great! You are showing me "he continued saying, after a short pause", that you are much more intelligent than you seemed at first. But I want to know something else, why have you denounced your comrade?

'Because I want to go back to England, sir.

The German frowned.

Go back to England? He was astonished, honestly.

"Yes, my lieutenant. I know that you are going to disembark in my country from one moment to the next. And I would like to return as soon as possible. I showed up before they called me up and I'm not old enough to be a soldier yet. I had to cheat, falsifying my documents.

"Were you so eager to fight us?

"It's not that," the young man hastened to reply. I was delighted, looking forward to the best adventure of my life. Unfortunately "and lowered his head, resting his chin on his chest", I was wrong from medium to medium ...

The tone of Slassen's voice grew warm.

"Don't worry, boy. What is your name?

"Justin Selby, sir.

"Don't worry, Justin. Everything will work out for you. I promise you that as soon as the German soldiers set foot in England, I will send you home. You are happy?

"Thank my Lord.

Now listen to me well. I've told you before that you are a smart and very observant guy. You are going back to the field. As if nothing had happened. You can count what you want. Namely...

His eyes sparkled in an unexpected way. He understood that the boy's return was going to pose difficulties for him. Therefore, approaching the door, he opened it ajar, shouting:

"Feldwebel!

Dietrich Klossen appeared moments later.

"You have to fix things," his superior explained, in German, "so that this boy is not in danger on the field. You know, the usual ... but don't hurt him too much. Have the interpreter explain it to you in detail, okay?

"Yes Sir!

Heinrich turned to the young man.

"Join the sergeant, Justin. He is going to give you some advice so that nothing happens to you in the field. And trust us. We are by your side. Nothing will happen to you.

"Thank you, my lieutenant.

Dietrich took him to a neighboring barracks and called the interpreter, explaining that he should tell the boy that it was necessary to hit him a little so that his companions could believe the story he was going to tell them. It was the only way to calm a bit the spirits of those who considered him a traitor. Pale as paper, Justin listened to the interpreter's words and then looked wide-eyed with fear at the sergeant approaching him.

"I won't hurt you too much, boy" Klossen told him, in German, with a cynical smile on his lips.

Then he started hitting him.

He did it scientifically, as he had learned in the SS. Fortunately, Justin Selby lost consciousness almost immediately, although the other kept hitting him. Then he called two soldiers and ordered them to take him to his barracks. As they walked away, Dietrich Klossen smiled at the dire state in which he had left the young prisoner. He liked to hit. It was something much stronger than him. And he hoped to do it on many, many more occasions, when he remembered, gnashing his teeth, the rebellious attitude of all the prisoners of Stalag XXIII.

The appearance of the Obertleutnant put his cruel thoughts aside.

"You're going to stay here" Heinrich told him. I'd like to take the car to visit Herr Funker. I'll be right back.

"All right, sir.

"You didn't hit him too hard, did you?

"No, my lieutenant. Just enough so that those pigs don't mistrust him. Have you commissioned any important work?

"Yes. From a very important one, sergeant. And now that I remember, tonight we are pulling a filthy Jew out of the barracks. Guardsmen haven't had fun for a long time. I hope they haven't forgotten what they learned, huh?

"They remember it perfectly, sir," Klossen replied. You can see for yourself tonight.

" I hope so! I don't want Jews in this field. We have had a lot of carrion by our side during these last months. Of course that Peter Fells, who is the name of the Israelite, does not know what awaits him ". He took a few steps away, then turned again to the sergeant. Then he said, "I was forgetting, Klossen. Distribute the ranch at about four o'clock. But don't let any of them leave the barracks. Take two men from each of them and have them distribute the food, but without anyone poking their noses out. Understood?

"At your service, Herr Oberleutnant!

Moments later, Heinrinch Slassen got into his Mercedes, giving the driver the address of one of the most important factories in the region. And as the vehicle passed through the gate of the field, Heinrich Slassen thought about the excellent brandy that Herr Funker would offer him, about the cigar that he would smoke at his side and, above all, about the profits that he could obtain if the powerful manufacturer accepted, as he thought. to do so, the collaboration of some five hundred prisoners, which he could assign to the smelting room.

Yes, he had been a truly smart man to leave the SA, at the right time. And despite having gotten rid of all those dangers, he could not help but shudder when he remembered that sad night, when Hermann Göering's armored cars surrounded the SA building in Berlin, driving inside and driving the leaders to that Munich prison where, weeks later, they left their cells to go directly to the wall.

Now it was going to be different.

Whether it wished it or not, the Third Reich rested on the SS, which had become the most important axis of the nation. The men who protected the Führer were SS, those who watched closely everywhere belonged to the SS. And even the Gestapo maintained close relations with the SS, which very often became its executive arm.

The Oberleutnant understood perfectly that Hitler did not trust the high command of the Army too much. He had had the occasion, while in Berlin, to attend a meeting in which the generals, with their ridiculous red braid running sideways through their khaki pants, felt superior, as if everything could be expected from them.

Bah!

Half of those pigs were already thinking of compromises with the West and had nothing in mind but plans to sign separate pacts, stopping the colossal war machine that had managed to make Germany the most powerful country in the world.

But they would have no choice but to obey the orders they received.

Near the Command Posts there was always some SS unit, which was called "protection"; but in reality, in addition to fulfilling that important mission, they were there to remind the generals that Berlin would not allow any betrayal, not even the smallest deviation from the orders emanating from the Headquarters.

And if anyone was insane enough to disobey, the SS would bring them to reason quickly, wasting no time. Because its men had become, neither more nor less, than the raison d'être of the new national-socialist state.

CHAPTER IV

In the last barracks in the row on the right, Marcel, sitting in the back, took off his dirty shirt, exposing his hairy belly, through whose hair he searched furiously, while biting his lip.

"Do they sting?" Asked his neighbor, a thin young man who gazed with admiration at the voluminous and hairy body of his bunkmate.

"Damn it!" Spat Marcel. " It must be a Nazi louse ...

"And what difference does it make?" Inquired the other.

The colossus and gigantic Santais looked at him with contempt.

"Ignorant!" He exclaimed. A French louse just bites; a Nazi gets into your blood to see if he discovers whether or not you are Jewish.

The young man smiled, showing meager teeth, although the few remaining teeth were white. The others jumped out of his mouth as soon as he reached the field, thanks to the knuckles of Sergeant Klossen's fist.

"What a grace! He exclaimed.

"I can't see her anywhere," growled Marcel. If it's a National Socialist louse, damn I'll catch it and then watch me pop it! "And continued rummaging in the fur where some white hairs were scattered, although scarce.

Claude then opened the bunkhouse door, stepping inside and carefully closing behind him. He was a thin, pale young man, with such narrow shoulders that they made one think, without mistake, of a characteristically tubercular chest, with exposed ribs and clavicles that left holes above them; holes that could easily fit an orange.

He looked back down the aisle of the feet of those lying on the straw. Then he dropped down next to Marcel.

"They have returned it to the field," he said.

The other seemed to have heard nothing and continued his search, until suddenly he laughed, pulling his broad fingers from the black hair, pressing the thumb and forefinger of his right hand.

"I already have it! He exclaimed, with a cry of triumph.

Claude looked curiously at the huge fingers of his friend and saw that the latter, with his other hand, seized the animal, taking it carefully and holding it up for all to see.

"It's a 'brown shirt! " He said ". See it, friends! A Nazi louse pig who has dared to suck the blood of a Frenchman! Damn you a thousand times! Now you are going to pay them all together you disgusting "brown shirt"! And you won't be able to call your "Führer" to save you …!

He placed the parasite on the broad, dirty nail of his left thumb and matched it with the same nail on his other thumb. The noise the animal made as it exploded was clearly heard. Then there was a brown and red stain, which Marcel cleaned thoroughly with his grubby trousers.

"One less! "sigh. Then, turning to the newcomer, he asked, "What did you say before, Claude?

"That they have made him return to the field.

"The... volunteer?

"Yes. They have brought it between two soldiers. Klossen must have taken care of him …

"Klossen! "Exclaimed the toothless, passing his fingers over his mouth, as if the German's name and the state of his teeth inevitably associated his ideas" The very pig!

"Hush" said Marcel. All of these are stories. They sure haven't hurt him too much.

"What do you mean?" Asked Claude.

"Which is pure camel. Don't you remember that he told the lieutenant that he wished to speak to him alone?

"Yes, but …

"Let me continue, Claude. That guy is a sneak and Klossen has disguised the truth a bit, to fool us.

"You mean he hit him on purpose, for no reason?

"Yes, that is what I mean. Have you seen him?

"From far.

Marcel finished scratching his belly and then tucked in his shirt.

"Listen" he said, looking at Claude. You're going to see the Englishman, that sergeant. Tell him I want to see him ... right now.

"Good," Duvillard replied, rising to carry out the order.

The colossus followed him with its eyes, a wry smile appearing on its lips. This gesture did not go unnoticed by the toothless, who said:

"They obey you, eh, Marcel? You have become the boss.

"Not yours ...

"No" replied the other. They don't fool me anymore.

Marcel smirked.

"You do well. You are too smart a guy. Truth?

The toothless man shook his head from side to side without much conviction.

"I do not take myself for clever" he said, but I am not fooled with your politics, Marcel. Your friends and the Nazis have signed a treaty. Have you forgotten?

" Fool! What do you know? But don't expect anything from us. And if you keep talking nonsense, you're going to have a really bad time.

"Have a bad time?" Laughed the other. What a grace! I see that you have taken seriously your role as leader of the Communists. After all, you are but a small group in the Field. Try not to forget it.

"We are few, but one of these nights we can twist your neck.

"I am not afraid of you. There are here, in the barracks, many who think like me and who despise you. After all, the difference between you and the Nazis is the color of the shirt.

Marcel was about to answer, but held back. Claude and the Englishman had just entered the barracks and the colossus quickly got up, without looking at the toothless, preferring to find another place to converse with the British. It did not interest him that ears as stupid as those of his previous interlocutor heard what he was going to say.

There was a place that the Communists had reserved for themselves, by the door. There were the eleven who served Marcel in the barracks, whom they respected and considered as their supreme leader. He didn't have to say anything to Santais to get the men to get up, forming a circle so that Marcel could speak calmly.

One of them stood by the door in case it was necessary to prevent the arrival of a sentry.

"Sit down ..." Marcel said to Adams. You speak French?

"Yes, quite a bit.

"Good. Best. I also know your language, but I have a hard time expressing myself in it. A cigarette?

"Thanks.

Marcel studied the Englishman carefully as he took the first pulls on his cigarette. From the beginning, and without knowing exactly why, she liked Shaw, with his strong body, boyish face, and the intense, luminous brilliance of his frank blue eyes.

"You were that guy's sergeant who volunteered, right? He asked out of the blue.

"Yes. Justin Selby was at my service.

"They have told me that they have returned it.

"That's how it is. But before they gave him a good beating ... I don't understand ...

"I do. Listen, buddy ... you haven't told me your name yet.

"Adams Shaw.

"I am Marcel Santais. As I was saying, what happened is crystal clear. That ... Selby must have gone off his tongue and the Germans beat him up when they realized that his act of volunteering for work had made us furious. It is about, neither more nor less, than having a snitch in the field.

"I don't think Justin is a traitor.

How can you be sure?

"I don't know, but I know him. He is a child who came to war deceived and who starts to cry when something fat happens.

"Just the kind of guys that Germans can make dance to the tune they like best.

"But what do you want that boy to do?

"I ignore it. Anyway, something said to the Nazi, let's see ... there are no communists among the men in your platoon?

Adams smiled.

"No, there are none...

"Good. And Jews, are there any?

"No, I don't think either ...

"Sure?

"Men! I'm not entirely sure, but no, I don't think so. Apparently you've been trying to make me believe that Justin is willing to sell out to his teammates.

Marcel's face clouded.

"Listen, Adams" he said ": you better know, now, from the beginning, that this field is divided into two groups. A very big one, that of the dreamer idiots, that of the guys who were born to be sheep and who let themselves be carried away as such.

"And the other group?

"It is smaller, but it is made up of men willing to protect the interests of the prisoners... waiting for better times.

"And you are one of the second?

"Yes.

"Communist?

"Yes.

Shaw shrugged.

"I was never interested in politics," he said. I am, just so you know, a professional military man, in a way.

"It does not matter. I'm going to tell you something, Shaw: I like you. I know you are a willing guy and although now it is too early to tell you certain things, there is something that may interest you ... later. But let's keep talking about that guy in your platoon. I want you to watch it. Do not trust him, and if you know that there is a Jew among your men, tell him to leave, there is a barracks at the back, empty. They died there, as soon as they arrived, sixty men with Typhus. The Germans removed the corpses and burned them, but they did not touch the barracks and none of them would dare to enter there again.

"I think you exaggerate; but, anyway, thank you very much for your advice.

"No, don't go yet. Tomorrow they will ask for volunteers for work again ...

"And good?

"Present yourself.

"Hey?

Marcel smiled.

"We will also introduce ourselves. We have been studying the case and I think we should.

"But don't you realize that the Germans have no right to make us work?

"Stop fooling around, Adams. You don't know the head of the Camp. Today he has not given us more than half a ranch. How long do you think it will leave us without food if no volunteers show up? Let the idiots starve! We need energy ... just in case.

Adams stared at the speaker.

"It seems to be" said "- that you have concrete plans. And I like that ... If you think they can be done better if we work, I will tell the boys to volunteer, as long as you do it too.

"We will set the tone tomorrow.

"Then okay.

Adams was about to get up when the door opened, giving way to Horace Colton, immensely pale, who looked up and down, then advanced on the sergeant as soon as he noticed him.

"Is something wrong, Horace? Shaw asked, full of sincere concern.

"They took Peter, sir! They have taken it! And I understood that they were treating him as a Jew ...

Marcel looked triumphantly at Adams.

"Didn't I tell you?" He inquired.

"It just can not be! But if that son of a bitch ...

And he gestured toward the exit. Quick as light, Marcel caught him by the arm.

"No, wait" he said. You are going to make a terrible mistake. It is precisely what the Germans expect ... Do not forget that they protect him and that nothing must happen to the snitch in your barracks. Come ... I'm going to give you something.

He carried it to the back of the hut, rummaging under the damp straw. He pulled out a wrapper, then checked that the toothless was snoring loudly next to them.

"Put some of these powders on that guy's ranch. And don't tell him anything, or scare him ... We'll take care of him.

Adams took the paper, then looked questioningly at Marcel.

"Poison?

"No" laughed the Frenchman ": jalapa. The latrines are at the back and that pig will have to go, tonight, to dislodge the guts. Don't say anything to anyone. Are your men suspicious of Justin?

"I do not think so.

Better than better. Go...

Adams looked at him in anguish.

"And the other? What will they do to Fells?

"You mean the Jew?

"Yes.

"You will see it tonight. They will invite us to the show ... they are very nice.

"But...

"Yes, don't get your hopes up any more. It would have been better if they killed him at the front.

Shaw's brow was sweaty when he left the barracks.

They distributed the first ranch at sunset. He had never spent hours so horrible as those, and when the prisoners entered the barracks carrying the cauldrons, Adams's hand in his pocket with the package that Marcel gave him trembled, clutched tightly between his fingers.

He had avoided looking at the straw where Justin lay, attended by Ed Cooper, who washed the wounds on his face and had placed a wet handkerchief over his companion's black eye.

How was it possible that this boy, a child, had been able to denounce Fells?

He shuddered.

They were dividing up the ranch and he made a gesture, indicating to the others that he would be the one to take it for the whole squad. Their plates had been taken from them when they were taken prisoner, but there were enough empty jars in the barracks for all of them, and Shaw and his boys had prepared one for each when they arrived.

Taking advantage of the fact that his soldiers weren't looking at him, Adams poured half of the powder into the pot that belonged to young Selby, but he couldn't help a nagging feeling while doing so, although he could avoid the worst after all if he could make sure of it. Justin's innocence.

He handed the boat to Horace.

"It's Selby's" he said. Give it to him.

Then he sat in a corner.

"If Marcel is not right," he thought, "he will go out with Justin every time he goes to the latrines ..."

What horrible world had he ended up in?

He had even forgotten his own problems and found himself, morally as well as materially, many miles from London. The image of

Deborah passed through his mind for a moment, but he pushed it away, as an insistent and annoying insect slaps away.

But what if Marcel was right?

He turned his head, staring at where Horace was feeding Justin, as if he were a child.

"We have just been taken prisoner" he said to himself ": we have only been here one day, and hatred, revenge, death, are already presented as important characters in this tragedy. Have we not suffered enough? What kind of horrors still await us? Is it enough that a group of men get together for the beast to manifest itself at once ...? »

The siren sounded then.

The men looked at each other and some began to protest, since they had not finished the slop that their boats contained. Moments later, a soldier was leaning out the door, yelling:

"Rauss!

"Go! "Someone said." Maybe they'll give us cigarettes and a cup of coffee with brandy ...

They all came out. Horace and Ed helped Justin, who was struggling. The men from the camp were gathering outside, and when they were in line, Sergeant Klossen led them to the first courtyard, next to the door that led to the section for the German barracks.

Peter Fells was there.

Two German soldiers framed him, rifles in hand. The searchlights cast a stark light onto the field, dramatically lengthening the shadows, which were grotesquely painted on the sandy ground.

Adams looked at the young man and saw that he was bare-chested and his head lowered. One of his hands rested on the handle of a pick. Frowning, the sergeant lined up with the others, standing at attention.

Oberleutnant Slassen appeared shortly after, turning toward the prisoners. A cynical smile would slightly part his lips. The interpreter walked beside him.

"I'm glad" said Heinrich, speaking slowly and letting the interpreter translate his sentences "to be able to provide you with the opportunity to see the treatment that National Socialism gives to Jewish dogs. Because this man, from whom we have removed the uniform that he did not deserve to wear, has fought against Germany, not like you, but hoping to offend us with his filthy presence ...

"You cannot understand all that we have had to endure to get rid of this filthy race. They stinked the streets of German cities when guys like this could move as they pleased, doing fabulous business when the German people were in need, under the misery that had been imposed on us with the "dictak" of Versailles ...

"They, the Jews, helped each other, dealing in everything, giving a damn about the misery and hunger we suffered. Some of these pigs dared to touch our women, sisters and girlfriends with their impure hands, taking advantage of their wealth ...

But Germany has awakened and is now ready to wipe out everything that smells of Jews! They are not even worthy of our prison camps! That is why I want you to see how I take care to prevent this filthy race from mixing with people whom it defiles and corrupts.

He turned angrily to the soldier:

"Start digging, Jew!

Klossen approached Peter menacingly, holding in his hand a club of the kind usually carried by Guardians.

Fells started digging.

A trench about six feet long by half width had been marked with chalk. He scooped up dirt until the edge was chest-high.

Then they made him go up.

The discharge from the submachine gun of one of the guards surprised everyone. As if pushed by an invisible hand, Peter Fells drew himself up, then plunged into the depths of his own grave, which he had done moments before.

"To the barracks! Rauss! Yelled the guards.

Ed and Horace had to carry Justin.

He had passed out.

I must have a fever ... Adams thought.

He was lying on the straw, wrapped in one of those thin cotton blankets that had been distributed to them and that smelled of carbolic acid, with which they were probably disinfected.

He shuddered every moment, but the fever "and he knew it perfectly well" was nothing more than a lie destined to deceive his own conscience, horrified not only by what he had seen at the beginning of the night, but by that vigil who imposed himself, aware of all the sounds that came to him from the place where Justin Selby was lying. "How can it be possible?" " he asked himself.

She had been listening to Justin, moving restlessly from side to side on his bed of straw. She also heard him sigh deeply and easily imagined the torture that poor boy must be undergoing.

"Poor guy?" "The angry voice of his conscience was raised." And Peter? He has died in an unworthy way, even ignoring that he had been denounced ... that a colleague, almost a brother, had denounced him ...

»

It disgusted him to have to think that way and now he remembered Marcel's words, when he referred to the Jew: "It would have been better if he had died from a bullet, in the front ...". How right he was! It was seen that the Frenchman had an experience that allowed him to know the truth, to intuit treachery where Adams would never have discovered him.

She heard Justin sitting up, complaining.

Then Horace's voice reached him.

"Are you feeling bad, Selby?

"A little ... I think I'm going to the latrine. My belly hurts a lot ...

"I will accompany you. You barely stand.

Unable to contain himself, Shaw sat up, glaring at Colton.

"Let me go alone, Horace! He "bellowed." Don't you know that Germans don't want to see two prisoners together?

A sad smile appeared on Selby's lips.

"The sergeant is right, Horace. Thank you anyway. I'll go alone.

"But you can barely stand up!

"I'll manage.

Ed Cooper had woken up and looked, wide-eyed but sleepy, around him.

"Something wrong? " I ask.

"No," Horace replied.

Justin was walking slowly towards the exit of the bunkhouse. Following him with his gaze, Adams couldn't help but shudder again. Sitting on the straw, Cooper sighed.

"'There's nothing to do! "He said". I can't sleep ... You fucking bastards! Poor Fells!

"You scoundrels! Horace confirmed.

"Shut up! "Roared the sergeant." Don't stir it anymore! He is dead and we can do nothing for him ... Besides "the tone of his voice softened somewhat. Now I could believe in Marcel ", I want to tell you something. Tomorrow they will ask for volunteers again. I want us to introduce ourselves.

"Hey?" Cooper was surprised ". Volunteers to work with those killers? Have you gone mad, sir?

"Do not say foolishness! They have killed Peter, it's true ... but someone reported him.

Horace's eyes widened.

"Report...?" he inquired, unable to believe what he had just heard. " Who could have done it, Sergeant?

Shaw gestured toward the bunkhouse door.

"It was Justin," he said, his voice muffled.

They looked at him, shocked and horrified at the same time. Sam Blue had woken up and heard the last words of his companions and the sergeant.

"That's impossible! He protested vehemently.

"It is true" replied Adams. Justin wanted to go back to England and, he very deluded, believed that the Germans would show up in London as they did in Paris.

"And the blows, were they thanks?" Asked Horace.

"They did it so as not to arouse suspicion among the other prisoners.

"I can't believe it," Ed assured.

Who knew that Peter was Jewish? Sam asked then. I did not know.

"Neither have I," Cooper said.

"Neither did I" intervened the sergeant. But Justin must know. Peter had more confidence with him than with all of us.

"It's true ..." Sam mused.

"No," Ed replied. I have read that the Nazis know how to discover Jews in the same way that we discover a black man ... They smell them from afar!

"Nonsense," Shaw replied. That will be in the cases in which the physiognomy of the Jews is faithfully portrayed; but, in Peter's case, they would never have found out. Fells must have belonged to a very mixed family for our race.

They were silent for a long time; then Horace said:

"It takes a long time. I'm going to see if something has happened to him. He's so weak and he's so small ...

"Still! Roared the sergeant.

"But...

"Do not move from here" he sighed then, lowering his eyes. There is something that I cannot explain to you now, but that I will tell you tomorrow. Come on, everyone to sleep.

She snuggled up in the squalid blanket and began to shiver again.

He felt infinitely tired, as if he had just traveled an endless road, through a bleak and cruel landscape. It was the first time in his life that he had acted truly wrong, since listening to himself would have prevented Justin from leaving the barracks. It was he who had pushed him into the darkness of the latrines.

Marcel's voice rang in her ears.

Don't worry, Adams. My boys will take care of him. All you have to do is add these powders to their food ... »

He shuddered again.

"I have a fever ..." "he thought.

CHAPTER V

On June 10, 1940, the situation on the French front was obviously chaotic. The German vanguards occupied a wide area that stretched from Dieppe, along the Atlantic, to Montmedi, on the Belgian border. Strong German motorized columns advance rapidly towards Rouen. Another has managed to cross Beauvais and is rushing, at full speed, towards the confluence of the Seine and the Oise, already a few kilometers from Paris. On the left wing of the German advance, the tanks were fighting around Soissons and further east, Reims was already shuddering as the assault tanks of the Third Reich passed by.

The French called their war, which was basically no more than a forty-day battle, with a special adjective: "drôle." The meaning of this word offers many others and it can be said that it would be translated by "funny", "ridiculous", "strange" and some other meanings more. The reality was that there was only partial resistance to the German advance and that very soon, since the collapse of Belgium, the Allied defeat was precipitated and there was nothing more to be done.

Two days were left for the final catastrophe to occur.

But on that morning of June 10, a man named Paul Sermaint, in his forties, was leaving entirely alone in a car, heading from Paris to the city of Orleans. If the ideas of that curious character had been analyzed, it would have been seen that the defeat of his country, which was already clearly defined, did not count exaggeratedly for him. Darker problems and much broader problems for him worried him at that moment. That is why, as soon as he reached Orleans, he went to one of the barracks where there were still soldiers who had not risen to the front. It was a quartermaster unit in which he soon found the man he was looking for. Marcel Santais.

Nor did it cost him much to obtain a permit from the chief officer of the company to which the colossus belonged and, half an hour after his arrival in the city, they both left in the car, without parting their lips until they met on the road he was driving. towards the south, on the way to Poitiers.

"I would have liked to find a few more," said Paul, glancing at his partner, but watching the road at the same time. " But it has not been possible. You will have to do it yourself.

"What is it about?

Sermaint did not answer, for the moment.

The road was full of refugee vehicles fleeing quickly from Paris. He had passed the formidable torrent of people who, even from Belgium, crossed France in those days of bewilderment and terror. But when they learned that the Germans were approaching the French capital, hundreds of people left their homes, taking only what was necessary and forming those very long caravans that the military police tried to channel, so that they would give way to the army trucks that were going up to Paris. .

But Paul, who was still silent, later showed that he knew the country perfectly, since he took a secondary road and was able to press the accelerator, not caring a damn about having to travel a greater distance, because he knew that he would reach Poitiers much earlier than if he followed the crowd. imposing of the people who fled and whose vehicles almost completely closed the road.

When he was able to normalize the car, he continued speaking:

"It is something very important, comrade. I have to go back to Paris as soon as possible, but I am going to drop you near the place where you will have to carry out your work as soon as possible.

"I hope you explain to me what it is about.

"Yes. I'm going to tell you. There is near Poitiers, in an abandoned mine, an ideal home where the army established a depot, many months ago. Arms, ammunition and grenades in incalculable quantities. A real treasure.

"Of course.

"Most of the men who moved all of that to the abandoned mine are at the front. Some will have been prisoners and others will be dead. Anyway, it is almost certain that they have forgotten the work that they did during that whole period of time that has passed from our declaration of war to the German offensive. Of course there is now a small garrison guarding the warehouse.

"How many?

"Five men and a sergeant named Courmont. I have tried to analyze what kind of types they were, but the reports I have received have not been satisfactory at all.

"What do you mean?

"That he is, as far as this Courmont is concerned, an old military man. He has even talked about blowing up the depot, if he receives orders to hand it over to the enemy.

" How funny!

"And we cannot allow that, Marcel. We are going through some truly important moments. You already know that I want to carry out the organization of a resistance group and that these weapons can be precious to us. Therefore, we have to seize them, be that as it may.

"You are not thinking of taking them out of the warehouse, are you?

"I'm not crazy enough for that. What I want is for you to finish off that little side dish. I've thought of you and was glad you hadn't come up to the front yet. I have not been able to forget that you were the instructor of destructions and hand blows in our cell.

Marcel Santais smiled.

"Thank you very much" he said later. Don't worry, Paul. I will manage.

"You don't think I'm going to let you go bare-handed, do you?

"Of course.

"In the back of the car case, there are weapons and explosives so you can do your job well. The place where that old abandoned mine is located is ideal for an attack. There is a small station opposite, which is not used by anyone. The railroad track is covered with dirt and trains haven't been around for ages.

"How did they carry the ammunition then?

"With trucks. Look, we're close ...

The landscape did indeed offer desert characteristics. A series of bare hills formed a small mountainous nucleus and it did not take long, following the road, to discover the old abandoned and useless railway that sank into those hills. Sermaint stopped the vehicle and got out, followed by his partner.

"It is there" he said, pointing to the bend that the train track was drawing. We should not get closer now.

"Agree.

Then they went back to the back of the car and Paul opened the suitcase, taking out a submachine gun and some sticks of dynamite, as well as hand bombs. They placed the small arsenal by the gutter and then Sermaint, staring at his companion, said:

"The sticks of dynamite are for you to blow up the entrance. I have brought you a small plan so that you know where you have to place the loads. A large land mass will fall and everything will be hidden.

"Are those guys inside the mine?

"No" smiled the other. I would have told you before. I see you had a great idea, right?

Marcel smiled too.

"It wouldn't have been bad to blow up the entrance and leave them inside. After all, they have to die ...

"But it is not possible to do so. They have built a small barrack at the entrance. As soon as it gets dark, you can come up and kill them. The rest will be easy.

"Understood.

"When you're done, you can go back to Paris. You know where you can find me.

"All right, Comrade Sermaint.

"Good luck to you.

"Thanks.

Moments later, Paul Sermaint got into his car and turned it around, driving away down the dusty road.

Marcel Santais was left alone.

Nervously lighting a cigarette, Sergeant Courmont turned to Pierre at his side.

"It sucks to hear the radio," he said.

"Of course. That is why I have closed it. Also "added the soldier, frowning," I can't stop thinking about mine.

"They live in Paris, right? Asked the sergeant.

"Yes sir. And they are alone. My wife, my two children and my old mother ...

"Let's hope the Germans do not enter Paris.

"It is an illusion, sir. Damn war!

"I would never have believed that things were so bad for us," continued Courmont, as if talking to himself. It is a shame that they have defeated us in this way.

"I wanted to ask something" said the soldier, staring at his superior.

"What is it about?

"Couldn't you give me a permit, in a couple of days? I would go to Paris and return immediately. Understand my impatience, Sergeant ...

Courmont nodded.

"I'll give it to you, boy. I just hope they tell us something about this ammunition depot. If we have to blow it up, we will and we will go. I would die of shame if they forced us to hand it over to the Nazis.

"Do you think they would order such a thing?

"Anyone knows!

The rest of the platoon was inside the second room that had the barrack. Pierre, who had been the first watch, stayed with the sergeant, since he had hardly been able to sleep for a few nights.

He was deeply concerned.

He could not understand, no matter how much he thought about it, how they had not used that formidable arsenal in the abandoned mine. He had heard on the radio that the French chiefs were complaining about the lack of equipment, and yet there were ammunition and weapons there for almost one division. He could not have the slightest doubt that treason had been nesting, since before the war, among the high command to whom the defense of the homeland had been entrusted.

And that made him frantic.

One hundred percent French, Courmont silently disavowed when tasked with guarding the depot. He would have wanted to go to the front, fight the enemy, as many others had. But, at the same time, a disciplined and obedient man, he stifled his desire to fight and clenched his teeth, but always waiting for the moment when he would be called to go to fight.

Night had fallen completely over the bare hills, covering them in intense darkness. Courmont and his men had grown used to the impressive silence that prevailed in the region away from where the mine was located. And if it had not been for the fatigue of the guards, they would have remained, as they did during the month of May, lying outside, on the thin layer of grass next to the railway, sleeping under the bright carpet of the stars.

In those moments, they could not imagine that a man was advancing, loaded with hatred, towards the barrack. They were so sure that they would not be disturbed by anyone in that isolated place that the guard was reduced, in reality, to a stay inside the barracks, a way of fulfilling military discipline in some way, although without much enthusiasm.

Who could get lost in those wild and abandoned places?

Marcel Santais advanced slowly towards the mine. Leaving aside the barrack, whose lighted window showed him that someone was awake, he went to the entrance to the ammunition depot and took there the sticks of dynamite that his colleague Sermaint had given him. The darkness was intense enough that he could not, for the moment, discern the precise shape of the mine entrance. But that mattered little to him. He planned to blast himself as soon as dawn, but first he had to do the main job: Eliminate the pesky garrison that must have been forcibly killed so that no one would know what had been hidden there.

He had no regrets at having to kill compatriots.

Party discipline had become second nature to him and he considered that obstacles to the organization's progress should be removed, in any way, without stopping to think about the personal consequences for those who should fall. in the silent struggle for a power that, with the German victory, seemed more distant than ever.

Moving amid complete silence, he approached the door of the barrack and clung to it, listening to part of the conversation that the sergeant and Pierre were having at the time. A fierce smile appeared on his lips as he realized that they were completely oblivious to the danger that lay upon them. It was easy to understand that these men, bored by the long stay in that remote place, were completely sure that no one appeared there. And that was going to facilitate Santais's sinister plans in a certain way.

His right hand lightly brushed the doorknob, checking, in a delicate and subtle movement, that it was not completely closed. Then, wielding the submachine gun hard, he gave the door a formidable kick, which flew open. He was used to this way of acting and did not allow the sergeant and the man who spoke with him the least time to react.

The submachine gun jumped in his hands as the projectiles came out and he found, at once, that he had not lost his aim, since the two men who turned towards him, surprised rather than scared, were lying on the ground, bleeding from their wounds. that the bullets had produced.

Someone shouted behind the door at the back of the room and Santais advanced, at full speed, knocking again the same way he had done with the front door. Four men were there, rushing to their feet, their eyes still half closed from sleep.

He fired again.

The French soldiers fell, writhing, unable to do anything to prevent this death that had come so unexpectedly. Seeing that one of them was still alive, Marcel approached him and, with all his cold blood, placed the barrel of the submachine gun less than four inches from the face of that unfortunate. Then he pulled the trigger and then had to withdraw so that the man's brain mass would not splash his face.

It was all over.

Thinking of the specific instructions Comrade Sermaint had given him, he found some cans of gasoline and set the barracks on fire, with the corpses inside. The best thing is that there was no apparent trace that there had been a garrison there, something that could make the Germans think of the existence of the ammunition and weapons depot. Then, checking that the light from the fire was widely illuminating the entrance to the abandoned mine, he took the map Paul had given him from his pocket and placed the charges in the places Paul had indicated. Several tons of earth were going to fall, blocking the mouth of the mine and thus hiding, until the precise moment, a treasure that could be translated into a further victory, when the resistance forces were appropriately organized.

Much earlier than he had imagined, thanks to the luminosity provided by the fire, Marcel Santais made the dynamite charges jump and went up the road, on his way to the road that was going to take him, later, to any point from where he could move to Paris.

But things were not also as he thought.

As soon as he had entered the French capital, eight hours later, he was arrested by a German patrol who disarmed him and without being able to reach Sermaint's home, they led him to trucks where, with hundreds of other prisoners, they took him north, making him penetrate into German territory to end up behind the barbed wire of the Stalag XXIII.

The foundry factory that Funker ran was located about ten kilometers north of the prison camp.

Oberleutnant Heinrich Slassen's Mercedes pulled up by the front door and the chauffeur rushed out of his seat, opening the door for his superior. He climbed the steps and entered the wide hall, where Funker's secretary was already waiting for him. The two men shook hands, then headed toward Funker's office, where the secretary left the military man.

Funker was a tall, thin man in his fifties. The blond hair that once covered his skull was almost completely gone, and the sunburned scalp glowed brightly. He had a broad forehead, which seemed much larger with baldness, and blue eyes, deep set in dark sockets that gave him a certain cadaverous appearance. He was dressed properly and rose from his office to meet the Oberleutnant, whose hand he clasped firmly.

"I was waiting for you," he said. Sit down please. A cigarette?

"Thank you" accepted the officer.

Obsequious, while Heinrich gluttonously smoked the Turkish cigarette he'd gifted him with, Funker went to a bar cabinet and prepared two glasses of real French brandy. He placed one of them along the edge of the table, next to the place where the officer was sitting, and then, taking the other in both hands, he spun it around, heating the amber liquid as he went to sit on the other side of the huge table. office.

"Have you done it yet? He asked, in a honeyed voice.

"Of course, sir," the officer lied. I did a little trial first, asking for volunteers, to see the result I got by treating those pigs like they don't deserve it. Naturally, no one showed up. But that is easily explained. They have been prisoners for a very short time and have not yet become accustomed to the duties they have towards the country that has captured them.

Funker frowned.

"I need you, Oberleutnant. You will see for yourself, in a few moments, my current situation in the foundry room. My teams of workers have remained in cadres, since many have gone to the front. In addition, speaking frankly, I prefer that dangerous work be done by those prisoners and preserve, at all costs, the health and physical integrity of our German workers. Don't you agree with me about this provision?

"Of course, sir. What happens to those pigs worries me little.

Funker smiled.

"Come with me now, Lieutenant. I'm going to teach you something funny.

They left the office and continued down a long corridor that led to a kind of gazebo, completely covered by glass. From there, at the feet of the observers, a very large room could be seen, one side of which was completely occupied by the blast smelting furnaces. The heat must have been unbearable in this room, since the few men who worked were in shorts and had the rest of the body naked. Their backs shone brightly with sweat and, from time to time, a reddish clarity gushed from the bottom of the ovens, subtracting from the whole an aspect that unquestionably recalled Dante's hell.

"It must be hard work," opined the Oberleutnant.

"Not only that," replied Funker. The really tricky comes when the furnaces have to be "bled". Although the facility is quite modern, we do not have enough equipment to protect the men and many of them suffer severe burns. The bad thing about it all "he added, after a short break" is that we have to work day and night, without being able to avoid it. I have already told you that quite a few of my workers have joined the ranks and are currently fighting on the front lines. For that reason, those men "and he pointed towards the room" are almost completely exhausted.

"Tomorrow you will have as many workers as you need, Mr. Funker" assured the officer. As soon as I get to the field, I will assemble the necessary teams. What would be the number of the first shipment?

"About two hundred would be enough for me, for the moment. Naturally "and he smiled in a cynical way", if you guarantee me to cover the casualties that occur.

"Of course.

"Then okay. Let's go back to the office.

Once they were seated again, after Funker generously served the French brandy that he kept in his bar cabinet, he approached the lieutenant and, smiling, said:

"I will give you two thousand marks a week, Oberleutnant. It looks good?

Slassen licked his lips before answering.

"Magnificent, sir. Thanks a lot.

"I have to give them to you, Lieutenant. He's going to get me out of a real bind.

"We all have to work, in our own way, for the march of the War Industry in our country.

"Evidently. Now, more than ever, we need to double the effort and produce as much as we can. If you read the Berlin reports, you would shudder to see the demands that are in all of them. I'm sure big events are in the works and that is why they need a truly fabulous amount of material.

"The war has only just begun" smiled the lieutenant. I also expect big surprises in Europe and, quite frankly, the one I look forward to the most is the landing in England.

"The day we crush Albion," said Funker, his eyes shining, "we will have at our disposal a heavy industry almost as important as our own. At this point, we will be practically invincible.

Slassen got to his feet.

"Now, with your permission, Mr. Funker, I am going to retire. I have work in the field.

"Perfectly, my dear friend. And if you need something, do not hesitate to come, with the assurance that if it is within my reach, I will provide it immediately with the greatest pleasure.

"Very grateful, sir.

"See you tomorrow then.

"See you tomorrow.

Moments later, the Oberleutnant's Mercedes left the factory grounds and headed out into the field.

Smiling, sitting comfortably in the back seat of the car, Henrich Slassen made calculations of all the money he was going to receive over the next few months. He hoped to get a lot more out, though, as Funker's needs increased. It was fortune, the goose that laid the golden eggs that fate had placed, gracefully within reach.

CHAPTER VI

As they entered the field, Slassen was immediately aware that something strange was happening.

As he got out of the car, Sergeant Klossen came to attention before him.

"Is something wrong, Dietrich? Asked the officer, unable to hide his concern.

"They killed the boy who came before you yesterday, Herr Oberleutnant," Clossen replied. Those pigs slaughtered him in the latrines.

For a moment Henrich was overcome with anger. But then, slowly, the light was on his brain and he even made a smile rise to his lips.

"Okay, Klossen" he said. I'm going to my office. Order all the prisoners to line up in the usual way.

Before reaching the building he lived in, he heard the whistles sounding, calling for the prisoners, and then the muffled noise of the people coming out of the barracks, on the other side of the second row of barbed wire. In his office, he did nothing more than collect the lists of all the confined in his Stalag, leaving later to find that all the prisoners were already, in the central street of the camp, lined up along the barracks.

The interpreter, as always, approached him, ready to take office. But this time, Slassen made a gesture to him, saying later:

"No, I don't need you now. I'm going to speak to him personally.

"As you wish, Herr Oberleutnant.

He went through the ranks first, staring at the men who never lowered their gaze. It was a challenging attitude, probably because they already knew or imagined that they were going to retaliate for the death of the snitch, murdered that night in the latrines.

"You are wrong," thought the lieutenant. But I'm going to show you how I tame the rabble of your class ... »

He positioned himself roughly in the center of the formation and raising his voice, said:

"I know absolutely nothing about what happened last night and the truth is that I don't care either. But I want to warn you that it would take me very little to find the culprit. Although, after all, I also despise snitches and, deep down, I think I would have done the same as you, if I was in your place. But let's leave that. I am going to ask for volunteers again for a job of great importance, in a nearby factory. Those who accept will have a higher general treatment than those who stay. I want to make an observation before: I want strong men, willing to fulfill the task that is imposed on them.

He paused.

"Of course this request for volunteers" he continued saying "is going to be a bit special. But this is a surprise for later. Now, those who wish to work, step forward.

He was completely sure that he would not get any results that way. For this reason, he was the first to be surprised to see about a score of men who came forward, taking that step forward and separating, therefore, from the general line that remained motionless.

Pleasantly surprised by this show of willfulness, he said:

"Magnificent! I see that there are, among this herd of pigs, real men who know their responsibilities. Feldwebel Klossen!

The sergeant came, standing at attention to the officer.

" Yes Sir!

"Take carefully the names of all those prisoners and their number. From now on, they will be considered as our friends and we will entrust them with special jobs, making almost all of them foremen. I also know how to be grateful. Now take them to the other part of the field.

"Yes sir.

The volunteers formed a line and headed behind the sergeant toward the barbed wire that separated the field into two relatively equal parts. Among them, of course, in addition to Marcel and his political party, were Sergeant Shaw and the members of his platoon. Adams had reflected on Marcel's words and, without being able to fully understand them, concluded that it was convenient for him, at least for the moment, to follow the instructions of that mysterious Frenchman.

After the volunteers had disappeared behind the horses that served as gates in the barbed wire, the Obertleutnant said:

"And now, the surprise that I had announced to you a few moments ago. Tell me, Feldwebel!

The sergeant obeyed, approaching one of the rows and beginning to count as he passed in front of the men:

"One two Three...

The prisoners remained motionless.

"...Four five six seven...

Motionless, but with bright eyes, the lieutenant watched the sergeant's advance attentively.

"... Eight ... Nine ... TEN ... You, get out of line!

The count was repeated, but when there were already five men outside, the lieutenant shouted:

" Tall!

Then he gave quick orders in German and the sergeant signaled, ordering two of the soldiers, armed with submachine guns, to approach him. When they were next to the group of prisoners who had been removed from the ranks, the sergeant said:

"Forward, towards the bottom!

The wide street limited by the barracks ended, in the easternmost part of the camp, in a high wall whose origin was inexplicable to the prisoners. Soon the five chosen were in that place and then yes there was no more doubt to those who were observing that and who could not help but shudder from head to toe.

Nor were the five wretches wrong about the intentions of the Germans. But they remained, where possible, calm, biting their lips hard even though their faces had paled in an intense way.

"Get up to the wall! The sergeant told them.

They did not understand a single word of what the German spoke, but it was not necessary. They obeyed, shuffling their feet, lowering their heads, not daring to look at their companions who, from afar, were following the scene anguishly. There was not even a need to follow the well-known process of executions. The sergeant had barely moved away from the front of the two soldiers, that his voice sounded like a whiplash:

"Fire!

Submachine guns barked and the men fell, piling on top of each other. A general shudder ran through the long lines of prisoners.

Moments later, the Feldwebel squared off before his superior.

"Order carried out, sir!

Slassen nodded, then raised his voice to say:

"I am going to ask for volunteers again. But if you refuse, I will seriously decimate your ranks. Understood?

No one answered him.

"Those who want to work in the factory, take a step forward.

The ranks moved in unison. They had all obeyed, with a shudder of horror, at the unheard of cruelty.

"I like that more" said the Obertleutnant, smiling and joyful at the victory obtained ". But I don't need all of you. The sergeant will select approximately two hundred who will head to the trucks tomorrow morning at five o'clock to be taken to the factory. He turned to the sergeant and added, in German, "Pick the strongest, Klossen. Then I ordered to break ranks.

"Yes Sir!

The first group of volunteers had been confined in a barracks, next to the second row of barbed wire, in a privileged place. Marcel was the first to be surprised to see that they now had sleeping mats and that the interior of the barracks did not offer the pitiful sight that the rest of the field did. Turning to Adams Shaw, he said, with a triumphant smile on his lips:

"You see that I was not wrong, friend. Glad you followed my instructions?

"Yes. You were right, Marcel. Have you been in this field for a long time?

"About three months. But enough to have more experience than you. I want to talk to you, come to the back of the barracks. We will settle on those two mats ...

Adams followed him and when they had settled in, well away from the rest of the men who, still excited by the shooting they had seen from afar, silently flopped down on their mats, Adams took a pack of cigarettes out of his pocket and handed one to the sergeant. British.

"This is just the first part of the pian" he said.

"What do you mean?

"That all this is aimed at getting us out of here. Haven't you imagined it?

"I suspected something, but not everything.

"You will see. I can't stay here, friend Shaw. I have a great duty in my country and I have to go back there, whatever it may be.

"Do you think we will make it?

"Of course. You let me organize things. I already told you that since I saw you I liked you. You are the kind of man one is safe with. It doesn't matter that you don't have my ideas. Little by little, as you watch us work, you will become convinced that the Party is the only thing that counts. And now I'm going to tell you something else: In France they await us. More eagerly than you imagine. Because there are many, many men who, barely without weapons, have to fight against the Nazis. I'm going to explain why ...

He gave her an account, in his own way, of the events that had preceded his capture in Paris. He told him about this colossal weapons and ammunition depot and then informed him that he had heard, in the field, that Comrade Paul Sermaint had been killed at the beginning of the occupation of Paris. This made him the only person who knew the location of the weapons and ammunition depot.

"Do you realize now? He inquired, staring at his interlocutor.

"That's very interesting," Shaw replied.

"Of course it is. There are hundreds of comrades who are waiting for those weapons. The deposit is truly fabulous. And don't think anyone is going to help us, at least for the moment. The English are very busy, and unfortunately the Soviet Union is too far away to help us out. That is why we have to show that we are capable of giving serious displeasure to those Nazi dogs.

"Count on me.

"And with your men?

"Too. They are all good boys and used to fighting.

"Everyone... except that pig Justin Selby.

Adams Shaw, unable to help himself, felt a bitter taste in his mouth.

"He was a poor bastard ..." he dared to say.

The other shrugged.

"He was a pig, a snitch, the worst a man can be in this life. Do you know who cut his throat?

"Do not.

"It was me, personally. Those guys disgust me!

But Shaw remembered Selby differently. In his imagination was the image of that poor boy, shy, full of fear, having made the mistake of introducing himself to, surely, surprise and be admired by the boys of the neighborhood where he lived. Of course, he had denounced Peter Fells and he had paid with his life for his partner's betrayal.

He stared at the Frenchman.

"You did well" he said. Fells was also an excellent boy.

Marcel gave him a friendly pat on the back.

"I see you learn fast, Shaw. You will be my right arm. And you'll see when we can face the Nazis, face to face. Then they will pay for everything they have done. It will be a merciless struggle, a relentless battle until the world ends up realizing that there is no other way out than the one found, after the First World War, by the people of the Soviet Union.

Before dawn the next morning, ten large trucks left the field and took the road that led to the Funker factory.

Before leaving, they had been given a truly extraordinary breakfast compared to the black water and bread of the same color that they were used to every day. They even distributed some cigarettes among the volunteer prisoners and there was a certain joy among them that was only stained by the memory of their comrades shot the day before.

Upon arriving at the factory, the interpreter, who was now accompanying Feldwebel Klossen, distributed the teams and almost all of the prisoners were directed towards the foundry room.

Others went to the railroad terminal to unload the scrap that was later to be melted down and turned into metal suitable for building weapons and war machinery.

Marcel and Adams were assigned, as foremen, to the foundry room. They soon realized the danger of that job and, above all, the horrible heat that reigned there. The factory was not really, a model that could be displayed to exemplify its genre. It was an old building that had been used for those purposes and that had nothing comparable to the very modern facilities located in other parts of Germany. There were three classic model blast furnaces and five modern Bassemer converters, with their characteristic pear shape and the pivots on which they rotated to pour the molten metal, unlike in the classic type blast furnaces, in which it was necessary to make the "Bleeding" ; that is, open the lower gate so that the metal can come out in a liquid state.

The sound that completely dominated the room was the roaring passage of compressed air, in the Bassemer converters, penetrating the nozzles to produce the proper oxygenation.

Once the equipment was distributed, the two new foremen had time to get away a bit from the torrid heat escaping from the furnaces and converters, standing at one end of the room.

"Now I understand why they needed volunteers" said Adams, with a sad tone in his voice. This is inhumane!

"It is not a marvel of foundry" replied the Frenchman, smiling. But don't forget that German workers worked here.

"But surely not in these same conditions.

"Of course. Anyway, you shouldn't worry too much. What counts is our plan.

For the first time since meeting Marcel, Shaw wondered if she had been wrong to join the man. He was beginning to realize that nothing counted for his partner except his own purposes. No, of course he would have liked to work with others, go through the same sacrifices and pains. And he noticed that his position as foreman was beginning to seriously annoy him.

But at the same time, the idea of Marcel, destined to reach France, filled him with irresistible joy. He understood all the good it could do when they were fighting the Germans. That was, without a doubt, the role destined for him. And remembering all the sufferings in that very long retreat, from Belgium to Dunkirk, he came to the logical conclusion that Marcel Santais was right to think only of the way to get, once again, to take up arms.

The first "sangria", made in one of the blast furnaces, impressed him. He saw that the men were opening the porthole and a white liquid, with a blinding shine, gushed from the bowels of the furnace, on the containers that later had to be transported by hand to the molds, using long iron bars to avoid touching the containers that quickly turned red. The Englishman looked fearfully at the men who, crushed under the weight, staggered from side to side, exposing themselves to the danger of the foundry falling and burning them alive.

It was a daunting spectacle, indescribable, capable of making the bravest tremble.

Bassemer converters, on the other hand, did not need to be 'indented'. When what was inside had melted enough, they turned on themselves, thanks to powerful pivots and complicated gears, pouring the liquid metal directly into the molds. But, nevertheless, the work carried out at high speed, without just a few seconds of rest, forced the men to a constant attention, running innumerable dangers in the midst of that torrid temperature that left the body without water, forcing the workers to drink constantly.

For a long week, they worked, surprised not to be sent back to the field. Indeed, some ravines had been set up next to the factory, surrounded by German soldiers and barbed wire, where the men fell exhausted after working for nine and up to eleven hours in a row. The shifts went on endlessly and it was hardly possible to sleep, or almost eat, since fatigue dominated everything. Meanwhile, Marcel was the only one who did not stop thinking for a single moment in the development of his audacious plan.

That afternoon, when they left the foundry, accompanied by their team as foremen, they were surprised to find the Oberleutnant at the entrance to the small concentration camp that had been set up next to the factory. The lieutenant smiled at him, distributing cigarettes and then offering him some bottles of alcohol that he handed directly to Marcel.

"We are very satisfied with the work of your men," he said to the Frenchman. But I wanted to warn you because tomorrow, around eleven o'clock, a colonel of engineers will arrive to inspect the factory. I want us to give you an optimistic idea of the progress of the work and I am sure that you will help me. It is not true?

Marcel smiled.

"Of course, sir. We are willing to collaborate in anything.

"I like it that way. You can announce to your men that we will distribute cigarettes every three days and that we will increase the butter ration in the mornings. I have also tried to make the meat ration larger. But you have to work tirelessly. You know, like me, that ovens cannot be turned off at any time.

"Yes sir.

The Oberleutnant dismissed them and then, already in his barrack, Marcel met, apart, with the British sergeant.

"Did you hear what he said? He inquired, his eyes shining.

"You mean about tomorrow's visit?

"Yes. It is the occasion we were waiting for. For something I have given instructions to Claude, who is the foreman who is now inside the factory.

"What instructions? Shaw was surprised.

"You will see tomorrow, my friend. Trust me. Marcel does not forget, not for a single moment, his purposes. Of course we will have to act at great speed.

"I do not understand you.

"Leave it in my hands. Now I'm going to talk to your men. They, with Claude, will be the ones out tomorrow while we receive an honorable visit from the colonel of engineers. Have you noticed that there are only eight Germans guarding our new camp?

"Yes, I have already noticed.

"It is not a very large number. Claude has been sharpening aluminum spoons and turning them into real knives. For something he worked as a metallurgist in Paris.

"Are you trying to attack the Germans with those primitive weapons?

"Of course. When we have worked inside the foundry, we will have a free field. For the moment, "he added," we will be forced to use two of the trucks. But then we will abandon them and I will be the one to direct them to the French border. It will be very hard, I know, but we have no other way out.

Adams could not help admiring the orderly and capable spirit of the man. It was clear that Marcel had received a special instruction, aimed at terrorist acts and hand blows. Once again his heart was filled with the idea of the freedom that he was going to achieve and, above all, with the possibility of being able to fight again against the hated German.

There were still some scruples in his soul, especially those that referred to the cruel and cold way that Marcel had to consider the lives of others, they were quickly erased, giving way to the illusion that allowed him to escape from that terrible captivity.

And Santais kept talking to him.

He was exposing the plan to him, little by little, keeping only the secret of what was going to happen inside the foundry. Perhaps the Frenchman had noticed the susceptibility of the comrade. The truth is that this was the case, and although Marcel appreciated the British, he did not cease to despise certain details in him that he clearly described as "bourgeois prejudices", being completely sure that he managed to tear them, definitively, from the heart of the English.

That night, Adams couldn't sleep.

The idea that the next day it would be very possible for him to achieve the long-awaited freedom had his soul in suspense. And for the first time since he was in captivity, he thought of Deborah again, cursing a thousand times the moment he had been fooled by this woman. It was as if the old wound was reopening, blood and pain gushing out. A tremendous bitterness seized him and he only managed to overcome it, almost at dawn, when the whistles called the daytime team and he had to get up, following his companions, on his way to the foundry.

Taking advantage of a moment, Marcel said, in his ear:

"Our day has come, friend. Today we will be free or they will bury us anywhere ...

CHAPTER VII

Arriving at the factory, Adams was surprised to find that Marcel's close friend, Claude Duvillard, was there. Actually, being the foreman on the night shift, he should have left the foundry. But it was clear that the Germans were increasingly trusting these voluntary prisoners, and that Oberleutnant Slassen had forced them to loosen their vigilance somewhat, since he was making huge profits from the work of these men.

Shaw could barely contain his impatience.

As the early hours of the morning passed, he realized the tremendous importance of the events that were to unfold soon after. And, walking next to Marcel, he kept looking at his partner out of the corner of his eye, wondering what details the other had hidden from him and that, in reality, they were going to be like the outbreak of the escape they were preparing.

Only once did Marcel go up to Claude, who had positioned himself next to the number four Bassemer converter. The two men spoke quietly and Shaw saw the other nodding vigorously. Then Santais approached the Brit again.

"Everything is ready" he said, in a low voice.

“I am impatient.

"It's natural. So am I. They are going to be important moments in our life, my friend.

And he smiled, but without his face showing any emotion. Adams had never seen a man of such coldness. There was a light of fanaticism that never left Marcel's eyes and that did not fail to cause his British companion some concern.

It was difficult for him to understand the way of being of a Latino, the way in which he felt his own emotions, the deep sense of his convictions that became, almost always, a fanatical expression of a feeling that would not bow to anything or anyone .

The morning passed much faster than Shaw himself had imagined.

And, suddenly, the doors of the room were opened and the British could see the arrival of the colonel of engineers, accompanied by a lieutenant of staff and by Oberleutnant Slassen, who was also accompanied by the director of the factory, Funker. The colonel was a tall man with a clear forehead, graying hair and an undeniable intellectual expression. He must have been in his fifties, but he marched in a martial manner, in his high gleaming boots and his uniform bearing the insignia of German Army engineering. Adams was somewhat ironic that this colonel wore spotless white gloves, amid the filth that reigned there.

"Don't say a word," Marcel warned him, in a low voice. I'll take care of everything. Understood, my friend?

"Yes.

While the workers continued to work, Marcel, after whom Adams was marching, approached the group of newcomers and then something happened that surprised even the British. Placing himself in front of the German colonel, Marcel saluted Hitler-style, raising his arm and throwing a heil in his powerful voice.

Pleasantly surprised, the colonel smiled and, turning to the Oberleutnant, said:

"You have achieved real wonders, my friend. I never expected that work was coupled with a national socialist sense in these men.

Slassen was in glory and shot Marcel a grateful look.

"I have never been wrong with men, sir

"He told the colonel." And in appointing this general foreman, I think I have not erred.

"Of course not. What's your name, boy? He inquired, fixing his gaze on the Frenchman.

"Marcel Santais, my colonel. On behalf of my colleagues "he continued saying" I welcome you and I hope that you find everything in perfect order, since we are willing to collaborate in the work that you have entrusted to us.

"Very well said", replied the colonel. Director Funker has already told me that production has increased considerably. Of course we will have to tighten the screws a little more.

"We are willing to make any effort," replied Marcel, undaunted. And now, colonel, may I invite you to see the emptying of one of the Bassemer converters. The number four. Will you do me that honor?

"Of course," the German replied.

So much cold blood on Marcel's part not only surprised Shaw, but he was also not surprised that his legs trembled slightly. He was sure that the invitation that the Frenchman had just issued would be the origin of the catastrophe that would unfold there moments later. Stepping aside, he let the Germans go ahead, preceded by the Frenchman, who led them to the huge converter, flames and sparks coming from its upper mouth.

Unable to avoid it, perhaps driven by a strange intuition, Adams surprised the gaze that crossed between Marcel and Claude, who had not moved from next to the converter, holding in his hand the lever that was going to make the enormous mass swing on its feet. swing doors. The four Germans naturally positioned themselves in a remote area from where the converter was to tilt to pour the liquid metal into the molds that some prisoners had already prepared. Certain that decisive moments were approaching, Adams was overcome by a sense of indescribable anguish and nervousness washed over him.

Because he thought that if something failed in Marcel's plan, they would end up, as Marcel had announced the night before, shot and buried in the vicinity of the factory. It was not, however, that he feared death, but that he could not conceive that things would turn out as well as the cunning Frenchman hoped.

The latter had moved away from the German group, tugging at Adams's sleeve, who followed obediently. Then, raising his voice, to control the thunderous hiss of the hot air nozzles, he yelled:

"Ready!

Claude Duvillard nodded.

Then he said:

"Yes, ready.

" Now! The Frenchman roared.

Claude hit the lever and the huge mass tilted; but instead of going to the side where the molds waited, the colossal apparatus swung sharply, and as it fell, swinging forward, it threw the roaring mass of liquid metal at the surprised Germans.

It was frightening.

The screams of pain, which could not last long, since the burns produced were going to cause an almost instantaneous death, dominated for a moment the roar of the liquid mass that fell on the ground. Being too close to the converter, the four French servers were also splattered by those drops of liquid metal that pierced their bodies as if it were the teeth of some voracious beast that devours the meat with great bites.

The sight of those bodies, corroding by liquid metal with indescribable speed, almost made Adams Shaw nauseous. But Marcel, on the other hand, had not lost his cool for a single moment. Approaching him, he said:

"Go! It's the moment!

They ran towards the exit of the foundry, while the other workers asked him what was happening. Of course, Marcel hadn't compromised with either of them and didn't give a damn what happened to them next. Only Claude followed him and soon they were out, running towards the esplanade, where the small concentration camp that had been set up for the installation of those who worked in the factory was located.

Arriving there, Adams realized that Marcel's plan had gone perfectly.

The three members of his platoon, Sam Blue, Horace Colton and Ed Cooper, in collaboration with members of Marcel's communist cell, had cleanly eliminated the sentries, with only one casualty, a small man lying on the ground, impaled still by the bayonet of his enemy that had fallen on him, with one of those aluminum knives stuck in his back.

They wasted no more time.

They went to one of the trucks and Marcel invited them to get into it, then got behind the wheel and started the vehicle, which sped out of that area, where the Germans had been eliminated, since the employees of the director's offices and assistants were completely unaware of what had happened.

Aware that every second had its price in gold, Marcel hit the gas and took a secondary road, following an itinerary he had previously studied. Three hours later they left the truck and went into a jungle area, moving through it without giving themselves the slightest rest. It still seemed a lie to Adams that this had all worked out. But he could not avoid, on many occasions, thinking about the revenge of the Germans and the reprisals that would be taken on those unfortunate people who, ignorant of the plan, had been left in the foundry with their eyes wide open, without understanding at all what was happening. happening.

Adams was never sure that they could get to France, as they did, without running into any serious obstacles. But that devil Marcel seemed to know all the paths and twists and turns of the border, and they only had a small encounter, with a couple of sentries, whom they cleanly eliminated.

Once in French territory, Horace continued to be the ideal guide and, hiding during the day, they walked at night gradually approaching Paris, where the Frenchman began to come into contact with the members of his organization.

Despite the fact that he could not forget what was undoubtedly going on in the concentration camp, after the events of that morning, Adams Shaw was sincerely glad to have led his men out of hell to give them a chance to fight. the Germans, weapons in hand.

Little by little, his apprehensions were disappearing, and when they arrived in the French capital, being able to sleep and eat normally for the first time, he understood Marcel's organizing genius and prepared to collaborate with him, perfectly convinced that he was a patriot one hundred. per hundred, whose sole objective was to fight against the common enemy.

They had been received in the popular neighborhood of Saint Denis by a family that, from the beginning, seemed to be completely under the command of Marcel. It was about a young couple who lived with their sister-in-law, a pretty beautiful blonde named Paule.

They stayed there for twelve days.

Marcel used to be out most of the day. Reunited with the members of his platoon, especially Sam Blue and Horace Colton, Sergeant Shaw spent long hours of animated talk, or was distracted by playing cards or chess, since it was completely impossible to leave the house, at least for the moment.

For his part, Ed Cooper had voluntarily separated himself from his friends, spending most of the day in the company of Claude and the other men who had managed to escape from Germany. Adams quickly realized that Ed was becoming as fanatical a communist as the rest of the people in the house. At night, when they met in the barn, where the blonde Paule brought them their food, Cooper's eyes were bright, his cheeks were flushed, and he used to talk non-stop, trying to convince his other platoon comrades.

He spoke with such passion that Adams was impressed, hurting him greatly that the young man had been carried away by ideas that he himself did not fully understand. They were, on the other hand, very far from satisfying him and the fact is that in his heart there was no place to consider men as mere numbers, much less to expose them to a dictatorship, be it black, like the one that dominated Germany, or in red, as it seemed to be the one that had been imposed in distant Russia.

"I don't understand you," Ed told him one night, as they all ate together. I used to think you were a man who loves freedom ...

Cooper smiled condescendingly.

"And I am, Sergeant Shaw. But not of that absurd freedom that until then has been the price we have paid for true slavery. Have you perhaps forgotten that deceptive freedom that, for example, in our homeland, is a kind of drug that they give us to put us to sleep and make us what they want?

"I disagree with you, Cooper. It is very likely that he thinks like you about certain abuses of the powerful. But you can't deny that freedom is the most beautiful thing there is. And don't tell me that there are various kinds of freedoms. There is only one. The rest is...

"You are very mistaken, sir," replied the young man, his eyes shining. There can be no healthy freedom as long as there are social differences. And this is what we want to achieve in the near future. Don't be fooled, Sergeant. This war does not have the same significance as the previous one and it is, fortunately, the first that is going to raise, in an indisputable way, the right of the most. I can bet you what I want that there will be profound modifications when this is all over. And men will realize that there can be no place for the slavery of the modern world ...

"Do you think it exists?

"Of course. A slavery, as I have said before, disguised as Freedom. The worst of slavery: the economic one. And while many are forced to pay for a false freedom the price of a life of work, poorly paid, living in indescribable conditions, a small majority do not tire of repeating those sheep who live in a happy, civilized world, full of promises and where individual Freedom is guaranteed forever.

"I still disagree with you, boy. Because I will always prefer to work for a man, to show him that I do it well, to get the necessary improvements from him, to be a slave of an omnipotent state, seeing myself forced to do what cannot please me, having in front of me a sad existence in which misleading words convince me or at least try that I am doing work for the common good.

Cooper smirked.

"You are loaded with prejudices, sergeant. But think about it. There will be no room for individualism when all this is over. The common good is above all other things. And those who do not meet the requirement of their enthusiasm for joint work will be eliminated.

"Nice way to express freedom!

Marcel's arrival cut off the conversation, which made Shaw happy.

"We can prepare" said Santais. Tomorrow we will leave Paris and head towards the central massif area. Our comrades await us there.

"And the weapons? Adams dared to ask.

"That will come later. We already have a plan to get hold of them. But, for the moment, we have to meet first with the group that is waiting for us, in the mountainous area of the central massif. In addition "and showed his teeth in a wide smile", I have the honor to inform you that I have been appointed head of that resistance group.

All of his friends surrounded themselves, shaking his hand warmly.

Adams, for his part, wondered again if he had chosen the right path. His two inseparable ones, Sam Blue and Horace Colton, remained by his side, taking no part in the jubilant joy that had taken hold of the others.

When he had finished shaking the hands that were warmly extended to him, Marcel approached the Briton.

"I want to talk to you, alone ...

"Whenever you want,

"Come under.

They left the barn and went to the room on the first floor where the dining room of the family that had welcomed them was installed. Sitting before coffee cups, the two men lit a cigarette and then, after a long pause, Marcel said ...

"I'm counting on you a lot, Adams. You have something that I lack.

"What are you talking about?

"You are a military man from head to toe. And that's what I need.

"For what?

"To seize the weapons. Don't think it's going to be easy.

"Are there many Germans in that region?

"Enough. Furthermore, that is not the primary problem. Moving weapons from Poitiers to the outskirts of Clermond Ferrand cannot be done without trucks. And we don't have a single one.

"We can get hold of some.

"That is precisely my plan. But I need a team of disciplined men and, above all, used to doing that kind of hand blows. Do you have complete confidence in your three soldiers?

"Complete; that is, in two of them ...

"Is there a new traitor? Marcel was alarmed.

"No, I do not mean that. But Ed Cooper seems to be more a part of your group than mine.

Santais laughed.

"He's a very clever boy, that Cooper," he said. He will be an excellent theorist. And we also need it. There are many men, in the resistance group to which we are destined, who need lessons in Marxism. Do you know that Cooper has asked me for a lot of books to illustrate?

"It was easy to foresee.

"It will become a top-notch agitator. I was lucky to meet you in the field.

"Yes, of course. And speaking of the field, what happened to those who remained there?

Marcel shrugged.

"Do you have scruples?

"It's not that, Marcel. But we should have brought them with us, at least the ones who worked in the foundry.

"Well you know that was impossible. We couldn't choose. Besides, you don't know men yet, my friend. There are many who do not deserve the slightest effort. They would then have become a useless weight that we would have had to bear up to here. No, forget it completely.

"I am trying.

"We have a formidable job ahead of us, Adams. And I know that you will collaborate intensely in him, by my side. We have to make the resistance group the first, the boldest, the most determined. There are things that I cannot explain to you yet, but then, little by little, you will understand them. I am not a man who plans for tomorrow, but for much later, for the future. The fate of France and its proletariat will depend, to a large extent, on the strength that we have achieved when the war is over.

"I don't want to get involved in political plans, Marcel. Do not forget that I am in a friendly country, but a foreign one.

"You must not think like that. The whole world is our country. But they are things that you will learn as events lead you to the path of truth. Now it doesn't matter how you think. Are you determined to help us?

"I am determined to fight the Germans on any terrain.

"It does not matter. Tomorrow night we will get out of here. It will not be difficult to get to where they are waiting for us, although we will have to open our eyes wide. Once there, you and I will carefully prepare the plan to go in search of the ammunition and weapons that will turn our group into the most terrible enemy of the Nazis. Together with you, with your military knowledge, we will prepare hand strokes and we will not let those invading dogs rest for a single moment. Although we will also have to do other things ...

He said no more.

Adams kept trying to answer, "in mind", to the hundreds of questions that his own conscience was asking him. But he got tired of doing it and, at the same time, he felt carried away by the enthusiasm of Marcel, who was explaining his future plans to him. Hadn't he wanted that? Didn't he want to continue fighting the enemy and turn off, whatever it was, the pain of the memories that, from time to time, broke into his aching brain?

The best thing he could do was to give himself, body and soul, to the mission that destiny seemed to have indicated. Fighting again was keeping your mind busy twenty-four hours a day. It was forgetting, above all that, and, at the same time, avenging those he had seen fall during the battle, on the way to Dunkirk. Make the adversary bow his head, feeling the weight of revenge, making him forget that proud and intolerable posture he had taken since the victory of 1940.

He looked frankly at Marcel.

"I am with you, my friend. I will do whatever it takes to assist the allies in the final triumph.

"I expected nothing less from you" smiled the other. I already told you one day that I was not wrong when looking at men. So far, we have not achieved more than triumphs and it will be so from now on. Soon the "Marcel" group will be heard all over France. And when they hear that word, the German pigs will tremble with fear because they will not know when we are going to fall on them, thus showing them that they are not, far from it, the owners of this land that they have violated, invading it.

CHAPTER VIII

They left Paris during the night.

A man had come to guide them to the mountains, and after crossing the city, dispersed in groups of two, trying to take those streets through which it was unlikely to run into German patrols, they left the French capital definitively, then climbing to a fish truck that drove them to Orleans.

Before reaching this city, they got out of the vehicle and crossed the river at a ford, some eight kilometers east of the town. Then they found the truck again south of the city and continued their journey.

Adams had noticed, with surprise, that the beautiful blonde from the house of Saint Denis, Paule, accompanied them. The trip was, however, tiring enough for them to take advantage of the moments when they were in the truck and they all slept, wishing they were finally in the mountains of the central massif.

At dawn the next day, the truck stopped in a mountainous, rugged and jungle area. Leaving it, always following the guide who preceded them, they took a path that snaked and ascended rapidly. Soon they lost sight of the road and found themselves in the middle of a forest of stunted and twisted trees, their trunks full of strange calluses, like monstrous tumors.

The path became more and more difficult and, finally, they had to walk on all fours, climbing cliffs that skirted deep chasms. Finally, already deep in the wildest area of the mountains, they were stopped by two men, armed with rifles, who shook the guide's hand and preceded him, leading him to a kind of small plain, cut on one side by a rocky wall in which some small caves had been excavated.

They were in the "maquis" camp.

The first thing Shaw saw, preceding a group of armed men, was a strange being, with a huge lump on his back and an unpleasant face. He was thin, with stunted legs and a skull of the same type. The curved forehead had a kind of dark line on its underside that formed the hirsute and terribly bushy eyebrows. The nose was flat and the eyes bulging. Under the first, the lips, thick and sensual, parted to reveal corrupted and yellowish teeth.

Marcel shook the man's hand and then, turning to the Englishman, said:

"This is my lieutenant. You can call him "Tordu." You won't be offended, I assure you. Besides, "he added smiling," I don't think anyone knows him by another name. Is not true?

The misshapen being nodded.

It clearly showed that the denigrating name did not bother him at all. Perhaps driven by some kind of dirty instinct for self-punishment, he was even pleased when everyone knew him and called him "Tordu."

"Did you do what I commanded you? Asked Marcel then.

"Of course. Do you want us to see them?

"Why not? "And turning again to the English, he said": Come with us, Marcel. There is something I want to teach you.

While the rest of the men fraternized with the newcomers, Marcel, the hunchback, and Shaw started walking away from the camp. This small plateau was almost completely isolated from the rest of the mountain formations that completely surrounded it. It was a kind of eagle's nest, and Adams, driven as always by his military spirit, said that the resisters had chosen precisely the ideal place, since the defense of this small plateau was easy enough.

Once they approached the edge, they followed a path that descended towards one of the valleys that surrounded that tiny plain. In reality, it was a terrace, produced by a cut in the mountain, leaving behind it the elevation where the holes had been made to turn them into caves. All the rest were cliffs and chasms, dangerously fringed by pointed rocks of undoubtedly volcanic formation.

They continued down the path until they reached the bottom of the ravine and once there, the hunchback turned to the right and led them to a small clearing, almost completely covered by lush vegetation, full of thorns. Turning to Marcel, he said, extending his arm:

"There you have them, comrade.

Adams Shaw followed the direction indicated by the "Tordu" and could not help but shudder.

What Marcel wanted him to see wasn't pretty.

There were, on the ground, covered in flies and dried blood, four men, their bodies clearly pierced by a multitude of bullets. Without showing the slightest emotion, Marcel approached, followed by the hunchback, until he stopped before the immobile bodies that lay on the yellowish earth.

"The very pigs! He roared. Then, changing the tone of his voice, he asked, "What did they say?

"Any! They were half dead of funk ... If you had seen them beg not to load them!

Marcel smiled fiercely.

Unable to contain himself, Adams stepped forward and, pointing to the corpses, inquired:

Who were they?

Marcel turned to him.

"The former leaders of the group, my friend," he said, still smiling.

"Did they do something wrong?

"The worst thing a man can do who fights against fascism. They did not fulfill the assigned mission. We had ordered them to go down to Saint Jacques, a town on the side of the road. They had an order to fill the guts of the mayor of that town with lead. And they did not. They said they didn't want to kill any French.

And that mayor?

Marcel spat on the ground, with visible anger.

"That mayor is one of the most disgusting collaborators in the region! A guy who has sold himself to the Germans. You'll understand, Marcel. Until recently, the people of Saint Jacques, as well as the people of the other town, which is called Villesud, also located on the road, had helped us, giving us food so that we could endure in the mountains. But the mayor of Saint Jacques flatly refused to help us and reported the case to the German town authorities. Two of our men fell into the trap and were tortured before dying. So "Tordu" sent those, two of whom were the leaders of a fraction of the group. But they refused to eliminate that scoundrel and, you see, they have paid for it ...

Shaw tried to understand what he had just heard.

On the one hand, his strict military sense told him that disobedience to a given order should be punished. But, on the other hand, he did not consider it logical to kill men whose fault had been to refuse to murder a compatriot.

As if reading her thoughts, Marcel said;

Think about it, Adams. If everyone did what they wanted here, our work would be nil. There has to be a discipline. Don't you understand?

"Yes. I understand.

"But there are other things that you will understand little by little. Unfortunately, not all the men who have gone to the "maquis" had clear ideas of the responsibility they accepted, when trying to fight against the invader. Many have done it out of snobbery, others out of adventure. And that cannot be allowed. The mission that brought us here is too dire to let some dream of becoming a stupid Robin of the Woods series. The French people are engaged in a fight to the death and there can be no room for cowards, traitors or the faint of heart.

Shaw had to give the reason, internally, to Marcel. He was always attracted to this man who had been able to prepare the blow for the flight from Germany in such a perfect way. But nonetheless, his old democratic instincts fought desperately within him, causing his conscience to say unpleasant things to him.

They left that place, returning to the camp.

Immediately afterwards, they gathered inside one of the caves and there sat the hunchback, Marcel, Claude Duvillard and the British sergeant.

"What interests us now, more than anything," said Marcel, "is to prepare the coup to seize as many weapons and ammunition as possible from the warehouse I have told you about. We have already said that the difficulty is precisely that we need at least a couple of trucks.

The «Tordu» intervened:

"That's why you shouldn't worry, Marcel.

"Do you have any idea? Asked this one.

"There is a German mobile park around Saint Jacques. Some of us have seen four brand new trucks in that place. On the other hand, the German garrison is not very large: six men and a sergeant.

Marcel smiled.

"That is what suits us. But I want the organization of this mission to be carried out entirely by our friend Shaw. As we have plans for the region and I know perfectly the path that will take us to the ammunition depot, we are going to study, if you think so "and he looked at the British", all the details of this plan. Naturally, you will be the boss.

They talked for a long time, examining the maps that Marcel had taken from his pocket and carefully studying the project that was to make the group of resisters the best armed in all of France.

When evening came and after having dined in the grotto, Adams Shaw went out for a walk, being surprised to see the "maquis" who, sitting on the ground, listened attentively to Ed Cooper's easy word, whose intentions went as far as the British sergeant, causing him sincere astonishment.

I would never have imagined that Cooper would be able to assimilate Marxist theories at such speed. The truth is that he spoke like a book and quoted things that Shaw had some difficulty understanding. He did not hear Marcel's footsteps approaching him and when the gigantic Frenchman was at his side, he said, smiling:

"You see, Adams. Your former private Ed Cooper has become nothing less than our best political commissar.

Shaw nodded and walked away, to the edge of the plateau. He wanted to be alone and think. But when he sat down on the ground, under the star-studded sky, he pushed all present concerns away from his imagination, and again, helplessly, he projected his mind into the past, as if he needed, at every moment, to return. to bleed for those wounds that a common woman had opened in his heart.

Two nights later, the group formed by Sergeant Shaw, Sam Blue, Horace Colton and Marcel Santais left the camp, heading towards the valley that was to lead them to the vicinity of the small town of Saint Jacques.

All of them were armed with submachine guns, had a pistol on their belts and some grenades hung in the same place. Marcel was leading the others and took the most direct route to get to the road. Once there, they moved along the ditch, silently, aware of all the noises that reached them. Little by little, they were approaching the town, stumbling before, as they expected, with the mobile park that the Germans had installed there, in a huge country house that was located about twenty meters from the road, joined to it by a dirt road.

Lying in the gutter, they carefully examined the house, almost immediately discovering the sentry who paced endlessly in front of the gate. A primitive hangar, covered with reeds, occupied the left part of the house and under it the greenish structures of the four trucks could be seen.

Lowering his voice, Marcel said to the sergeant:

"Now it's your turn, Adams. What is your plan?

"I'm going to personally take care of the sentry," Shaw replied. As soon as he has eliminated it, we will all go into the house and finish off the rest of the Germans. Only by eliminating the entire garrison can we get the trucks moving and, at the same time, take advantage of the Nazi uniforms and documentation in case we meet someone on the road.

"Have you noticed that when the alarm goes off, they will look for us everywhere?

"I have counted on that. But once we are at the ammunition depot, where we will arrive as you have calculated in a couple of hours, it will not be difficult at all to change the registration number of the trucks and thus be able, on the way back, to go unnoticed. In addition, you have also said that we would take a side road to reach a point where those of the group would wait for us to take care of everything we have loaded. It is not like this?

"Indeed. I like your plan. You can start whenever you want.

Stepping out of the gutter, Adams Shaw crawled slowly toward the sentry.

It was as if he was back on the front lines again, and all the memories rushed into his brain, abruptly. He had completely forgotten the special circumstances that had him there and saw himself transferred back in time, like when he was advancing on patrol, knowing that he was protected by his men and sure of himself, like any man who fulfills a duty towards which he thinks he is obliged.

The sentry kept marching from one side to the other, completely oblivious to the danger approaching him. A master of the art of approach, Shaw moved forward, creeping cautiously, keeping an eye on the silhouette of the German, whose bayonet gleamed from time to time when he turned sharply after his walk was over.

When he was close enough to the German, he sat up, preparing to jump. He had grasped the submachine gun in both hands and planned to deliver a final blow to his adversary that would put him out of action, with as little noise as possible. But the silence that reigned in the house was significant and clearly demonstrated that the rest of the garrison were enjoying a deep sleep.

From a deep and eternal sleep from which he would never wake up.

He jumped, precise, down a path he had foreseen in advance.

Raising his left arm slightly, he caused the submachine gun to make a semicircle and its metal stock to crash brutally into the German's face.

He gasped, then suddenly doubled over, landing heavily on the ground. The helmet had fallen from his head and Shaw, aware of the danger of his regaining consciousness, raised the submachine gun again and struck, brutally, on the skull of the unfortunate.

There was the dry sound of bones breaking and a posthumous shudder ran through the German's body.

Then he froze.

As he headed for the gate, Adams heard perfectly the footsteps of his companions approaching rapidly. The door was not closed and they pushed it carefully, making sure that its hinges moaned as little as possible. Inside, there was a kind of wide patio with an abandoned cart on the right and some farm implements that were already rusty, thus showing that the owners of the house had long since abandoned it.

It was not difficult for them to orient themselves, finding a staircase that led to the upper floor. They climbed it, weapons at the ready, carefully stepping on the edges of each step, taking care that the wood did not groan under the weight of their bodies. Once at the top, they ended up in a corridor, with doors on both sides, all of them ajar and some of them letting out the characteristic sound of the normal breathing of a person sound asleep.

Distributing his men, Shaw entered one of the rooms where two Germans slept. Acting in the same way that he had used against the sentry, he struck the skulls of his adversaries and then went out, verifying that the others had done the same with those who slept in the neighboring rooms. Death had come silently and quietly to the house, which seemed still sunk in a peace that, in truth, was for its occupants of the moment, definitive and eternal.

Leaving the building, they then went to the garage where they checked the status of the trucks. They chose two of them, which they went through carefully, filling the tanks with the gasoline cans that were there. Then they went back to the building and, now allowing themselves the luxury of turning on the light, they chose the uniforms that best suited them. The most difficult thing was finding one that would fit the colossal dimensions of Marcel Santais, who finally got the largest, although the warrior's cuffs did not reach much lower than the elbow.

Smiling, he said:

"I will hide inside one of the trucks. I don't think anyone would be convinced if I told you that these clothes have shrunk when I washed them.

Sam Blue smiled.

The two vehicles started up shortly thereafter. As Marcel had assured, they were able to take a secondary road, five miles above the German post they had just attacked, turning left and entering an area where it was visibly unlikely to run into enemy patrols.

It did not take them more than two hours to travel the distance that separated them from that little forgotten station where Marcel, so many months ago, had finished off the French garrison so that the secret of the ammunition depot would not be known to anyone.

The remains of the barracks he had burned were still visible, but when he got out of the truck, running towards the entrance that had been blown up with dynamite, he roared with rage.

The others approached him.

The entrance was clean, open, showing that they had dug there and that someone had therefore discovered the secret.

Using the flashlights they had seized at the German military post, they penetrated inside to convince themselves that the weapons and ammunition had disappeared.

Marcel's eyes seemed to threaten to bulge.

"Now I understand! He roared, clenching his fists.

"The fact that? Asked Shaw.

"It was that traitor of Paul.

"The man who ordered you to blow up the entrance?

"Yes. I know he died, but he was cowardly enough to sell the secret before he died.

What if they have tortured him?

"So what? He roared again. A Party member must not speak, even if his eyes are gouged out and his meat cut to pieces. Damn it a thousand times! If I had suspected that he would not know how to keep his tongue still, I would have strangled him right here, burning him next to the corpses of those I had to kill so that the secret of this warehouse would not be known to anyone.

"And what do we do now? " I ask.

"Get out of here" said Marcel. We will go back to the trucks and burn them, before we get there. Dammit! We are back as before, with a few submachine guns and a handful of bullets. And we haven't even taken the weapons or ammunition from the Germans in the fleet. But who knew that this surprise awaited us here?

"We can go back there if you want," Shaw said. There were a dozen rifles and two boxes of ammunition.

"You are right. It's something. Let's go.

They got back into the trucks and Marcel, sitting inside one of them, pressed his lips angrily, biting them at times, until he made blood.

He had counted so much on making his group the most important in all of France that now, full of spite, he wanted to take revenge on anything, let go of the brutality that was inside him and unleash the hatred that welled up from every one of his pores. Little by little, as they approached Saint Jacques again, an idea crossed his brain causing his lips to part in a cruel smile.

"At least" he thought ", we will not have wasted the night ..."

CHAPTER IX

Seizing the weapons and ammunition from the house occupied by the German fleet was simple, since the alarm had not yet been given and that had a logical explanation. The German garrison was located at Villesud, twelve kilometers further south, and this motorized detachment was the only German group in the vicinity of Saint Jacques.

When they had crossed the road, on their way to the mountain, Marcel stopped suddenly and said, turning to the others:

"You can continue to the camp. Claude will guide you. Then, staring at Adams, he asked, "Can you let me have one of your boys, Shaw?

"Naturally. What do you want to do?

"I'll tell you later. Designate the one you want to accompany me.

"See yourself, Horace" said the Briton.

Colton handed over the weapons he was carrying, dividing them between Sam and the sergeant. Then, silently, she followed Marcel and they both drove off, crossing the road again and taking the ditch, then moving toward the quiet little town of Saint Jacques.

It would have been frankly difficult for Horace to understand the feelings that were then nesting in Marcel's wild heart. The truth is that he had not been able to forget for a single moment the failure of finding the abandoned mine empty, where the ammunition and weapons should have been, especially after the sacrifices that keeping the secret had cost.

A primitive man, but at the same time endowed with a remarkable natural intelligence, one hundred percent astute, Marcel Santais could not suppress, in any way, the vengeful spirit that nested in his chest.

Burdened with resentment towards society, having suffered the unspeakable in a hazardous youth, in the most miserable neighborhoods of the French capital, he was now suddenly converted, for the first time in his life, into something important. And the responsibility of his position seemed to impose on him the need to demonstrate to others his ability and his lack of mercy towards those he considered enemies. He quickened his pace, followed by Horace, who carried his submachine gun on his back. He did not say a single word during the journey and when they reached the entrance of the village, he raised a hand, signifying that they should stop.

"Take the submachine gun in your hand, boy" he warned.

Horace Colton did.

"Are we going far? He dared to ask.

"No" replied the other. We are already very close. Follow me and fear nothing. Here in Saint Jacques, there are no Germans.

Horace nodded his head and followed Marcel, who had started walking down a narrow, silent street with a strong smell of manure, demonstrating the existence of stables in almost every house in front of the streets. what was happening. The street was badly paved and Horace had difficulty walking, in his boots, because of the round, slippery edges that, on the contrary, his companion seemed to dominate completely.

They walked about a hundred yards, then stopped by a small door that led to a fairly high wall. Right next to it, Marcel worked with the knife until he managed to pop the old, moldy lock that was more of a symbol than a sign of security.

"Come on," he said, with a whisper.

The garden they passed through was wide, and Horace smelled the fruit that must have been suspended from the trees, the tall shapes of which surrounded them.

The ground was covered with a layer of soft earth that was a pleasure to walk on. When they had reached the back of the house, Marcel repeated the same maneuvers that he had done earlier on the garden gate. He seemed to have an extraordinary ability to jump locks, and moments later he put the knife away, then turned to Horace.

"Now try to make as little noise as possible, boy" he said, in a low voice "Hit yourself and me and don't get too far apart. I will guide you. Understood?

"Yes," replied the Briton.

To further increase his proximity to the man before him, Colton reached out and took hold of Marcel's warrior. In this way, they both advanced in complete darkness. But, apparently, the Frenchman knew perfectly the topography of those places, since he did not stumble even once, finding the staircase very easily, by which they began to climb to the upper floor.

Complete silence reigned in the house.

As he followed closely behind Marcel, from whom he had freed himself as he started up the steps, Colton wondered what they were going to do there and who the inhabitants of that house were. But he didn't have much time to reflect, and when they met on the first-floor landing, Marcel headed right, tiptoeing forward, with chilling assurance. Colton followed him and moments later they stopped in front of a door that, contrary to the previous two, was not locked.

Santais's hand moved, groping, along the wall until it found the switch. The stark light forced Horace to close his eyes, though he opened them quickly, curiously examining the room in which he stood.

It was an old-fashioned, classically French, oversized bedroom with a huge wardrobe on one side, a table in the center, surrounded by some chairs and a couple of armchairs covered in a flowery fabric, and at the bottom , a marriage bed in which two people slept.

Fixing his attention on those two human beings, Horace felt uneasy, uncomfortable, as if entering the matrimonial room constituted some kind of violation, a positively reprehensible act. They remained that way for a few moments, Marcel, with an ironic smile on his lips, cautiously advanced towards the bed where the husband and wife were still sleeping peacefully, oblivious to the unpleasant surprise that awaited them.

Turning around the bed, Marcel approached the place where the man slept and then appeared, as if by magic, a knife in his hand. Horace could not contain a shudder although something told him that his partner was not going to proceed violently against the person he was getting closer and closer to.

Indeed, Marcel merely shook the sleeper by holding the knife close enough to the other's face to signify that any alarm would simply be fatal to him.

The man grunted a couple of times before opening his eyes. Then he struggled a bit with the vivid light in the room, and finally his eyes fell on the knife to see the sleeve of the arm that held it and, finally, to open in a disproportionate way when he looked at the face of the man who was standing next to him. bedside.

It was then that the woman woke up.

Scared, she sat on the bed, putting her hands to her chest to close the already tight blue shirt she was wearing. She was a rough woman, rude, fat and without any trait of beauty. She opened her mouth, as if to scream. But Marcel then brought the knife to the throat of the husband and the wife understood, easily, what that gesture meant.

"Surprised, huh? Asked Marcel.

The man had also sat on the bed and was shaking in such a way as to give pity. Horace grew more and more self-conscious, wondering anxiously what the immediate future events would be. He was looking at the woman, feeling ashamed of having caught her in bed, next to her husband. That is why he preferred to turn his head to fix his attention on the two men.

"What do you want...? The man stammered.

He must have already reached fifty years of age and his hair was white, although short and shaved, with some black spots that formed curious islands in his alb. He was as fat or perhaps more than his wife, and his flabby flesh was now moving at the impulse of the tremors that ran through his body.

"And you still have the audacity to ask me what I want? "Laughed Marcel". You liked the show of our two dead comrades, right?

The man struggled desperately to get his lips to articulate the words he most certainly wanted to say. He finally got it and said:

"It was not my fault, sir. It was the Germans.

"But you reported them, dog. You killed two of my best boys.

"I swear it was not my fault! "Begged the man, whose face had somewhat taken on color, although the pallor was still cadaverous.

Then the woman intervened.

"My husband is telling the truth, I swear. We were not to blame for what happened. It was the Germans ...

Marcel seemed to react in a deeply human way. Keeping the knife away, but still smiling, he said:

"It's okay. I believe you. Now I need your wife to prepare enough food for this friend and I to take supplies to the camp. Understood?

It was the woman who answered:

"Of course, sir. Right now I'm going to prepare it.

"You will do well" laughed Marcel. But if you don't put the best you have in the pantry, your husband is going to have a very bad time.

"Don't worry, sir" she hastened to say, as she jumped out of bed, hurrying to put on a colorful robe that made her even more ridiculous and fat than she was ". I'll take the best we have. There are still a couple of hams, plenty of bacon, sausage and chorizo, cheese ... you like that, don't you sir?

"Yes, I really like it. Come on, hurry up. "He then turned to the British." You accompany her, Horace. And don't lose sight of it. Do not forget that the daughter must be sleeping in a neighboring room.

"Alice will not wake up" intervened the husband.

Horace then followed the woman out, more self-conscious than ever. He did not like this way of procuring food and did not understand much what Marcel had spoken, since his French was quite elementary.

Still, it disgusted him to see fear painted like that on the faces of human beings who, after all, shouldn't have done much harm to anyone.

They had just come out into the corridor when a door opened, next to the room they had left moments before. A girl in her twenties, in a rather pretty dressing gown, which further enhanced the beauty of her childish face, with her large, wide-open blue eyes, appeared before them, fixing her gaze, somewhat frightened, on the armed man who accompanied him. to the woman.

"What is it, mom? " I ask.

"It's nothing, Alice. These friends of your father have come to look for some food for the maquis. I'm going to pack a good package for you. Come on, come with me!

"And dad?

"He's talking to the other gentleman. Nothing happens, don't panic. Come with us.

The girl obeyed.

She glanced at Horace and continued to do so, even when they found themselves in the vast kitchen, helping her mother less than she should have expected of her. It was so long since Horace had been in the vicinity of a beautiful young woman like this that, helplessly, he felt a chill run down his spine. There was, however, in his intentions, absolutely nothing sinful. He looked at the woman as an extraordinary object and found her completely different from Paule, that woman who was also beautiful but a bit of a tomboy who was with them in the camp. What a huge difference there was between the two!

Fear gradually left the face of the young woman who, animated by the admiration she was being subjected to, smiled, approaching the Briton.

"Won't you have some coffee, sir? " I ask.

"I don't know if we'll have time, miss ..." Horace replied, in his lousy French.

"I'm going to do it. It is a matter of a few moments. So when your friend comes down, they'll take it together.

Colton, without stopping to contemplate the girl for a single moment, thought of the strange fate that he had made of those people, creatures sunk in constant terror, fearing on the one hand the Germans and on the other hand the men of the mountains, without knowing which way to go or what attitude to adopt in that savage fight that completely enveloped them.

For an Englishman, war could never unfold that way. For this reason, Horace understood the combats, the fights, but nevertheless it was difficult for him to understand that special state of affairs that made human creatures frightened beings, living in the midst of an unrest so unspeakably frightening that it was horrifying just to imagine it.

Apparently, Marcel was entertaining with the husband of the owner of the house, since the girl had enough time not only to prepare the coffee, but to help her mother fill those two sacks, in which they had placed the best that was in the cupboard.

Shyly, Alice brought the cup closer to where Horace was still standing.

"Have some coffee" she told him, with a charming smile on her lips ". I have made it loaded and very sweet. Likes it like that?

Horace nodded his head and reached out, grasping the mug and feeling a strange sensation as his fingers brushed against the girl's delicate skin. His heart beat faster than usual and he had to make a real effort to keep her from noticing the trembling that had seized his hand.

He sipped the coffee, sipping it with real relish. The two women looked at him and there was a sympathy in their eyes that never ceased to fill the heart of the British soldier with joy.

But then, when everything seemed so enchanting that it seemed impossible, an ideal pursued endlessly, uselessly, when things had taken on an unreal aspect, when it seemed that past and present, memories and images of the moment had coincided in one go. Perfectly, Marcel's harsh voice sounded from inside the door:

" Come on boy!

Horace hastily set the mug on the edge of the table and turned. He did not like the smile on the Frenchman's lips. He then walked over and glanced at the sacks the two women had filled.

"Come on" he repeated. We have a long way to go.

He threw a sack on his back and was followed by Horace. Then the woman approached Marcel, her eyes pleading.

"And my husband?

"Your husband has come out to give orders so that they prepare more food. I'll send more men in a couple of hours. Come on, Horace!

They left the house, then crossed a square and took the direct path towards the mountains. Although they were going fast, the silence of the night was so deep that it was possible, moments later, to hear a scream of terror that reached them, through the blackness, as if something unspeakable was tearing itself apart.

"What was that?" Said Colton.

"Nothing, go on.

"What do you mean nothing? It sounded like the girl's voice.

"I told you to go on.

When they began to climb the slope, Horace could not help it and turned, seeing then that many lights had been turned on in the town. Seeing his partner's gesture, Marcel smiled and said:

"They will have already found out.

"The fact that?

"Mayor.

"Was it the man in the bed?

"Yes. The very pig denounced the Germans who were coming this way and they killed two of our men.

"What have you done to him? Horace inquired, feeling something rip inside him.

"Nothing in particular. I have hanged him in the main town square."
Colton had to bite his lip.

And he didn't feel the pain, not even the taste of the blood flooding his mouth.

* * *

Major Shelton pointed the map to the colonel.

"It must be around here, sir," he said.

Colonel Freedman carefully observed the contour lines, which met, almost met, thus demonstrating the topographical structure of the terrain.

"It's natural," he said, after a pause. This place is excellent for maquis.

"We have no true report, sir. But we will have to risk it.

"Of course. Anyway, why don't you take a flight in broad daylight? If they saw him, they would signal and thus we would know the precise place where to make the launches later.

"It's a great idea, sir.

"Do you want to go out tomorrow?

"Of course, my colonel. I also prefer to know the exact site. Later, during the night, when we launch, we will not have as much security as during the day.

"Of course.

"I will prepare my aircraft and fly tomorrow, in the early hours, over that area of the Central massif. Too bad we don't have informants in that region!

"It does not matter. If, as we think, there is an important group of resistant people in that area, they will see the colors of the device and understand that we want to help them. The time has come, my friend, to start arming those good patriots. If we want to get a landing one day, we have to have friends in the interior of occupied France. And there are many. You know that in the Netherlands and Belgium we are in communication with important groups that will help us, when the time comes, for a productive collaboration.

The supplies that I had made, months before, to the resistant nuclei of Holland and Belgium demonstrated the effectiveness of those men who fought in the shadows without ever giving in, eager to make the Germans understand that things were not and would not be as they wished. .

After meditating for a long time on all this, Shelton began to write a letter to his wife, announcing that very soon he would have a permit and would be able to go to London, to spend a few days in her company and in that of the two children he had. marriage. Generally dedicated to observation, Major Shelton knew the dangers of enemy fighter, but did not have to endure the insistent action of the German antiaircraft like his companions, those who were assigned to the bombing squadrons. After all, he thought as he wrote, it was lucky, and besides, I like this job more than the other one. If there is something I cannot bear, it is the idea of having to bomb cities, without any precision, knowing that under the bombs there will be innocent children, women and people who have done nothing wrong in this life.

The next morning, he got on his observation device and shortly afterwards it flew over the English Channel, heading southeast and reaching a height of seven thousand meters, an area in which he could fly almost completely calmly. In addition to him, three men made up the twin-engine team, which was equipped with all possible advances in aerial photography. But this time, the mission was different and Shelton, while driving the plane, thought of the joy it would bring to those men who, in the mountains of France, could not imagine that someone, on the other side of the sea, was waiting for them, eager to help them in a positive and effective way.

CHAPTER X

"English! It's an English plane!

Marcel went to Adams, along with the other members of the platoon.

Except Ed Cooper.

"What do you think, friend? "He said, putting his hand familiarly on her shoulder." Compatriots of yours! It's nice to see you!

"It's true ..." he said, with an emotion that constricted his throat ". I didn't think I would ever see them again. As if they did not exist "he said, after a short pause" ... as if they had disappeared forever.

" What are you saying!

"It's true, Marcel. There are things that seem to disappear from our soul in a definitive way. They were so far away! In another world, even though reason said otherwise.

"Look! Now they parachute something ...

Indeed, an object had just detached itself from the plane, a blinding arrow in the rays of the sun, halting its fall as the flickering flower of the small parachute opened.

"Pick it up! Marcel yelled.

England exists! Adams thought. It is not some vague idea of mine: it is something true, material, visible and palpable like a beautiful woman ... »

The object was hit by a Frenchman who then ran towards Marcel, making the little parachute fly on his tail, like an open handkerchief fluttering in the wind.

"Here it is! He said, handing it to his boss.

"Open it," he just said.

"What does it say? Santais asked.

"We wish to help you by sending weapons and ammunition, which we will parachute in two nights. Tell us if you are happy to mark, with lights or small bonfires, a ring to indicate the place of the launch. We are proud of your fight against the Nazi enemy. England salutes the brave fighters of the French Resistance.

»We will also launch you a station and a password so that you can communicate information or ask us what you want. Now light a fire to let us know that you have understood. Cheers, friends! Long live France! Live england!"

"That's it," Adams said.

"Magnificent! We are going to light the bonfire right now. Hey y'all!

When the plane saw the plume of smoke rising from the ground, it tipped its wings in salute, drifting away as it soared into the high clouds.

"What luck! "Exclaimed Marcel." You see they don't forget us, Adams. These Englishmen are really nice guys.

"It's true.

"You don't seem as happy as you should be.

"I wanted to talk to you. Do you want to come, Marcel?

"Of course!

They stopped by the ledge. Adams sat up, being followed by the other.

"You will say ...

"It's about last night.

"I do not understand.

"Yes. Horace told me everything.

"And that?

"Understand, Marcel. We are grateful that you got us out of Germany, but we do not understand why you have to be so uselessly cruel.

"Bah! Sometimes I wonder if you English people realize what kind of war we have to carry out here. By all the demons gathered! Did you want me to leave the deaths of two of my men unpunished?

"The 'Tordu' killed some of the group's comrades.

"They were traitors!

"No, you are not fooling me, Marcel. I've talked to your men. You killed them because they weren't from the Party.

Anger made Santais clench his fists.

"What if it was for that? He inquired defiantly.

"If it were like that, as it is, I would tell you that things cannot continue this way.

"What do you mean by that ...?

"You have already seen that the English are going to help you. But if they knew that they were playing the game to a political idea, if they really knew the intentions of this group, do you think they would help you?

"Are you trying to tell me that you are going to inform them?

"I will, Marcel. Unless all this changes. You have no right to kill members of the group because they do not think like you, much less to hang civilians, who must be tried, at the appropriate time, after the war.

Contempt was painted on the Frenchman's face.

"It sucks to hear you talk like that! But tell me one thing: before you entered the army, what did you do?

"It worked.

"Where?

"In London.

"In what?

"He was a commercial agent.

"Already. An apprentice bourgeois. An element of that disgusting middle class who is starving but doesn't want to be noticed. Puah! Realize, my friend: you were just a worker, no more, no less. A guy like there are millions in the world and for whom we want to fight. Is that a bad thing?

"Do not. I understand the fight for the betterment of men. Don't forget that I live in a democracy. But that's all very well by the time the war is over: now, Marcel, our goal is different.

Santais creased his lids, narrowing his eyes. Under the skin of his face, the muscles contracted.

"You may be right" he said.

"Then?

"Agree.

"Will the executions in the group stop?

"They will cease.

"Will there not be more revenge against the civilian population?

"Do not.

Adams held out his hand to the other, who shook it.

"Count on me then. Because you should know that I am a radio specialist. It's one of the things I learned in the commands.

"Magnificent! I am never wrong and I knew that you were going to be of great use to us.

The men, French and English, were distributing the fires to signal to the British planes the place of the launch. It was not really more than a previous rehearsal, since there were two nights to go before the scheduled date.

"Paule!

"Did you want something?

"Yes. Let's walk away I want to talk to you.

"Good.

"Listens. There is something serious that you could help us solve.

"What is it about?

"From Adams.

"A handsome man" he said. How I like them.

"I am glad that it is so.

"Why?

"Pay a little attention, Paule. Shaw disagrees with certain of our procedures. He is an Englishman, don't forget it. As candid and fanciful as all the English. Able to say that he had to wait for the war to end, for example, to hang the mayor of Saint Jacques.

"Delicious! And now that I remember, why didn't you take me with you? I told you I wanted to play a trick on him before you hung up on him.

"I could not. But let me continue. You need to take care of him. You have to distract him, whatever it may be, take him away from our things so that he doesn't play us.

"Are you afraid that he is a traitor?

"No, nothing like that. But he's going to become station manager and I don't want him to send "personal" reports to London. Do you undesrstand now?

"I think so.

"We don't give a damn what happens to England after the war. Our mission is not going to limit itself to driving the Germans out of here, but to establishing a Soviet socialism throughout Europe. That is why we are interested in receiving many weapons and ammunition that will not only be used against the Nazis, but that we will use later, if necessary, against the British and Americans, if they want to impede our purposes.

"I agree.

"Then you will realize the need to neutralize Adams.

"But, what can i do?

" Do not be stupid! Cooper has told us a lot about the sergeant. Did you know that he was married?

"Do not.

"Well be surprised. He entered the army in disgust, with a broken morale. His wife cheated on him before and after he was.

"And that's why the fool got desperate?

"Yes. But that's beside the point. Do you think you can divert him a little from what we do not want him to know?

She smiled, feline.

"I don't think it's very difficult. Also, you just gave me some very interesting details for a woman. It will have to be caught by the romantic ...

"Do whatever you want, but make it asleep as much as you can. It is vital to us.

"Do not worry.

"When are you going to start?

"Right now. Where is that Othello?

"Down with the men.

"Leave it on my account. I still haven't forgotten what I learned a long time ago, before I discovered that all men are pigs ... delicious.

Marcel laughed.

"All right, comrade. It is the Party's mission. Do not forget...

"No, I will not forget.

And he got to his feet, moving away towards the area where those who were open on the road and that the unions had organized so that the mass did not lack stimulant along the way.

How much fun they had and danced that day!

There was no shortage of the accordion that was playing without interruption, carrying the popular rhythm of the «javas», which followed one another endlessly, causing the couples to raise dust and turn their cheeks red until they looked like fire.

They came back very late. The stars shone in the sky and they continued singing and dancing through the already quiet streets, stopping from time to time to gleefully stick out their tongues at those who leaned out of the windows to protest this noisy scandal.

It was impossible to remember certain details. Especially what they had done. With an effort, Paule tried to pin down this point, but to no avail. The truth was that things had lost their usual appearance and that it seemed to him that all objects were surrounded by a luminous halo that gave them a new personality, as if they had ceased to be what they were to become living, animated, friendly creatures. , smiling ...

For instance...

Who had shed light on the Seine? How was it possible that the lanterns in the lighting looked like men in formal clothes lighting a cigar?

How funny!

In addition, someone, without a doubt, had pushed the ball of the world and the streets and squares moved, swaying to the beat of the music that rippled in the air the tireless accordion.

A boy said they should keep the party going.

"Let's go to Michel's garage! He exclaimed. We cleaned it up the other day and it's great to keep dancing ...

Everyone applauded.

Something seemed to break in Paule's chest now, as she continued down the hill, in search of the British sergeant. It was as if someone had just dropped a crystal goblet on the floor and the vibration of each piece continued to resonate as it crashed.

From that moment on the memories were vague, perhaps because the heart flatly denied that they could have been reality. It was the moment when he had to inevitably open the old chest in the attic.

They danced, they drank; they drank, they danced. The world shattered into chunks of light and everything was spinning, dizzyingly, but without looking annoying or uncomfortable. Quite the contrary: a voluptuous sensation of immateriality seized her, making her lose contact with her body, as if she had sprung wings and was no longer more than a piece of music that the accordion released like luminous streamers.

Later...

The memories made their way, painfully, one by one, as if someone were pulling his hair, viciously, cruelly. The world had stopped turning and the boys turned into bold, hard, strange hands, into breath that did not detach from the face: a sour breath, dominated above by the hateful shine of those eyes that seemed to be releasing lots of sparks

It was like a wind of indescribable violence. Stirring around, screaming, their eyes streaked with tears, the faces were parading next to hers, always with brilliants that seemed to be the same; always with that sour stench that seemed to come from the same bold and shameless mouth ...

It was ringing? How long had you been chatting with Adams Shaw? It's that he ...

Do not! Do not!

It couldn't be the same. Unable to separate the present from the past, his crazy mind mixed everything up and he even seemed to hear, against the background of an imprecise cloudiness, the sound of the accordion deflating, wavering from an air full of notes ...

He opened his eyes.

The stars were in the sky like tremors of light. The silence settled, heavy, unbearable, on his chest. However, there was a pleasant perfume in his mouth, like the one that remains after having smoked a blond cigarette to the end.

A part of the sky was covered when the head of Adams appeared. It was impossible for her to see him well, but the outline of his face was perfectly outlined against the distant blue of the sky.

"Paule ...

Why did he have to speak now? Didn't she realize how delicious it was to be carried away by that invisible current that had taken her away for the moment from the pains of a past that she wanted to forget in any case?

"Paule ...

The man's hand rested on her hair, his fingers tangled in it. The fingertips brushed her temples and she felt an artery throb under the pressure of the man's skin on hers.

She sat up, sitting on the ground. Now she could look at him in greater detail.

"Paule ..." he repeated, obsessed with something. "Me...

She smiled at him.

She was still under the influence of something new that, in an unlikely way, had confronted her, for the first time, with herself. How was it possible, after so many bitter experiences that were nothing more than a mud bath on mud?

She looked at him, interested, as if she were capable of discovering something in his face to explain that wonder. Everything, absolutely everything, had suddenly been erased, as if he had just come out of a cleansing bath, something similar to something he read or heard, but which he could not specifically remember.

He again made the mistake of breaking the silence, which was the bottom of the bewitching charm that seemed to envelop her.

"Sorry, Paule ...

River. But he did it without malice, as if he wanted to hear his own voice, as if he feared waking up from an unreality that he had not even dared to imagine during all those years. Then suddenly, realizing the certainty of what had happened, she threw herself at the man, seeking refuge in his strong arms.

"Adams! Protect me!

"But...

"Don't let me go, Adams. Do not let me go...

He stroked her hair and she, her face pressed to his face, spoke to him, in a low voice, like a whisper, telling him everything as she had never done it to anyone. And now, going back in time, he no longer felt the dreadful apprehension, as every time he went up to the attic to lift the heavy lid of the chest, expecting to see the snakes and spiders in the background. Then she told him, clearly, Marcel's intentions and the role he expected her to play alongside the Briton.

Adams was still stroking her. From the entrance of the cave, where the radio station had been installed, Adams could see the men, under Marcel's command, rehearsing the weapons that the English aircraft had parachuted into successive nights.

Paule slept inside the cave.

Turning to her, Shaw couldn't help a smile. How many times had he wondered how it had been possible that the presence of that woman, who seemed vulgar when he met her, had extinguished the flame of pain that never ceased to accompany him.

Would the communication of pain and suffering be necessary for the light to emerge? I did not know, I did not know it.

But the truth was that both had come out clean, when approaching they carried the burden of their own misery. Paule knew his life now as he knew the woman's. They had undressed without false modesty, eager to see if the path they had just discovered was, after all, nothing more than a fleeting mirage.

"No, it isn't ..." Adams mused. It has been wonderful and definitive. Curious! Something as if two lepers, rubbing their wounds on each other, had even disappeared the pustules and the disease.

He saw Marcel coming up the slope, approaching him. He had been wiping his forehead and then sat down next to the Englishman, taking a cigarette from one of the packages that had been parachuted at them.

"Is there news? " I ask.

"Do not. It's still early. They will arrive tonight.

"Do you have the request list?

"Yes.

"We, the group, are going out. All.

"Yes?

"Yes. We are going down to bring some reports. You have to pay for what they are doing with us. Don't you think? We are going to blow up the road and the bridge, in front of Saint Jacques. Nice hit, huh? Remember that many Nazi convoys are passing now, heading for the area that they have the shamelessness to call "not occupied."

"Tell London that we are going to start attacking everywhere. As soon as we can, we will go to blow up the Villesud iron bridge. Isn't that a good idea?

"Excellent.

"I'm going to prepare all the boys. Do you want me to leave someone on guard for you?

"No, it is not necessary.

"Good. See you tomorrow!

"Good luck to everyone!

"Thank you ... Abur!

Half an hour later, as the sun set the orange hues of sunset on the hills, the long line of men moved away, down the valley.

CHAPTER XI

They were moving toward the road when the Tordu came to a halt, ordering most of the men to hide. Then he went to the place where Claude, Marcel and Ed Cooper were waiting for him.

It was Cooper who was calling the shots.

"I tell you, comrades, that we cannot become mercenaries of English capitalism. It is true that they send us weapons; But do you think they are doing it out of benevolence or because they care something that France is free from the occupier?

"How? "Asked 'Tordu'". Don't you want the Nazis to leave here?

"I didn't say that! Cooper replied. Of course I want it; but for what? To save their beautiful island and their empire, to continue to rule the world as they have done until now. No, comrades, we have to prove to our false friends that we are even smarter than they are. We will continue to receive weapons and do, from time to time, something that satisfies them. But our true mission is to start sowing communism in France. When I waved the red flag here, I tell you that my old England will have to surrender to the evidence and millions of Indians and people from other subjugated countries will find the way to freedom.

"Cooper is right" Santais said. Not for nothing, on your advice, I had Comrade Paule entertain the sergeant. Adams is a good boy, but he is poisoned by bourgeois prejudices.

And what should we do? Claude chimed in, who hadn't spoken so far.

"It's very simple," Cooper replied. Our mission is to cleanse the surrounding villages of fascist traitors, of collaborators of the Germans. By doing so, we will earn the trust of the French workers, who will be attracted to the Resistance and will join our ranks.

Little by little, we will form a considerable force that, when the moment of liberation comes, will definitely prevail. It is necessary that when the English arrive in France, they do not believe that their victory will mean the prolongation of the same state of affairs that until now has exclusively favored them ...

"How he talks! Exclaimed « Tordu ».

"Formidable! "Corroborated Marcel." You've come up with a great guy, Ed. And we all agree with you; but I see something that is clear.

"The fact that?

"If we dedicate ourselves, as we all wish, to cleaning up the Villesud collaborators, your two companions, Horace and Sam, will run to tell Adams. How to avoid it?

"Very easily. Send those two idiots, along with some of our comrades, to kill the Germans in Villesud. Didn't they tell us that there would only be eight or ten Nazis left in the garrison, since the rest were going to a parade to Vichy?

"It's true.

"Well, you already have a wonderful opportunity to distract those two while we settle the scores with the traitors of the town.

"You think of everything" Claude admired.

Moments later, the column was on its way, moving along the ditch, toward Villesud.

The stars shone, trembling, in the sky. Were they capable of reading the violence that men carried in their hearts?

Paule stretched lazily. She was lying next to Adams, who, with his hands behind his neck, his eyes narrowed, allowed himself to be carried away by the calm and calm course of his ideas.

"When I was a child," she said, playing with her long hair, "she believed that the stars were holes in a huge blanket that fell to the earth at night. It's curious! All that my grandmother told me, who also made me believe that the moon was capable of lowering to punish men.

"Moon?

"Yes. My grandmother was Breton. Actually, my family comes from that region. They are simple people, deep believers, but loaded with dark and remote superstitions ... very curious.

"Like that of the moon?

"Yes. Do not laugh. It was something that excited me so much that I spent the nights shivering when the moon was out and I begged my mother to close the window tightly.

She lay down next to him, stroking his face.

"You'll see. My grandmother told me that there was a man who was riding a bullock cart through the fields. It was night and it had rained a lot. The cart was loaded and the animals fought bravely to save the puddles whose mud bottom made the wheels spin.

"Suddenly, what was supposed to happen happened. One of the wheels got into the mud up to the axle and the shouts of the carter were of no use, nor the blows of the goads that he gave to the poor oxen. The man, tired of futile fighting, sat on the side of the road and took out the bottle of wine. It was then that, defiantly, he looked up at the moon and full of rage, he exclaimed:

» " I invite you to drink if you help me get the cart out of the mud!

And then the moon came down and took him away. The next morning, the cart arrived in town, completely clean and with the oxen rested and shiny. People wondered where the owner of all this could have gone and when night came, the oxen bellowed lamentably and raised their heads towards the moon. There you could clearly see the silhouette of the man who wanted to associate with the powers of the Demon.

"Didn't you see that human silhouette, Adams?

"Silly!

"I know it's a lie, but at that time I was fully convinced and I saw the man on the pale face of the moon, shaking with terror.

He twisted his head, looking at her.

"You are wonderful, Paule.

"Do not say that! Do you want to make fun of me?

"No, darling. For me, you are the most beautiful thing in the world. Understand it. My heart was bleeding and you came to show me that it was not true, that it was all a lie.

"You have fulfilled my wishes too, Adams. It happened to me just like you and I had taken refuge in hatred because it was the only thing that was offered to me for free.

"There must be something" he said "that takes care to bring together those who complement each other, when they can no longer believe in anything or anyone.

"Yes it's correct.

"What does the man ask after all, Paule? A bit of happiness, a corner where to forge a home, a possibility of life, tiny, barely perceptible. Can you imagine now what all the soldiers in the world think? It is the same that you look from one side to the other. They all revolve around the same thing, little one. They want to go home, be with their loved ones, forget their miseries and sufferings.

But they can't. And do you know why? Because they have been poisoning their minds for as long as they can remember. They say to the French: "He hates the German! He killed his father, he hurt your grandfather. They are a warlike people, eager for power, destructive." They tell the German that he is a superior being, that the French expect the An opportunity to humiliate him again, that the whole of Europe despises them.To us, the English, they speak of the empire, of our educational and guiding mission in the world, they convince the American that he is the youngest and most powerful race on Earth.

»Poisons that do not stop falling on the child, on the adolescent, on the man! How few are those who teach that we must love others, that they are our brothers, that it is not necessary to kill each other savagely to agree!

Why are we not able to understand the beautiful truth, Paule? What demonic power gets inside us to turn us so easily into ferocious beasts?

"It's hate, Adams.

"Hatred? But do you think that someone can hate for himself? It is impossible! It takes a little imagination to see that it is not true. Look at it, little one. If we were now able to move time forward, do you know what we could easily see?

"Do not.

"The war is over. A long time has passed and the French go on vacation to Germany, like tourists. So do the Germans, who wander through Paris, where the traces left by the Nazi occupation have been completely forgotten. You realize?

And that is precisely what saddens me. Realize the stupidity that each generation seems willing to commit. Wars end, people run through the streets, hugging each other when they have achieved peace. Crossing the no man's land, those who yesterday interbred, hug each other excitedly, kiss, distribute cigarettes and drinks. Where is that hatred that just a few hours ago made them grit their teeth as they fiercely pulled the trigger?

»No, Paule. They are generous, able to forgive or understand. But twenty years later, they will again shout hoarsely in the streets, curse neighboring countries, and prepare to go to war.

Who is to blame for all this? " I ask.

"And what do I know! Sometimes I have believed that the politicians were responsible, but I have seen them tremble and wish for peace, as happened before 1939, when our minister was dragging himself at Hitler's feet.

"He is to blame for everything!

"It is not possible, Paule. How could one man just unleash such madness? No. Hitler would only fail and end up in a madhouse if those around him, his people, reflected a little, just a little. But his poison-laden words find an echo in the hearts of crowds, in the same way that it has happened thousands of times, throughout history.

And it is quite possible that we are too gullible and stupid, despite boasting of superior civilization. That's what happens, little one. Every human group has its lie, its great lie, which it desperately clings to, fully convinced that it is true. Each generation puts on the stage of the world several great lies: Capitalism, Communism, Fascism, National Socialism, Liberalism, Democracy ... Gigantic lies that poison and lead to war, hatred, destruction.

It is as if each man was condemned at birth to live in the great lie of his century. For this reason, surely, when a man grows old, he becomes skeptical and it is no longer possible to draw him into the enthusiasm that these lies arouse in his youth.

"For you, my love, the moon was capable of descending and taking a daring man. It was the great lie of your childhood years. I have also suffered another lie, believing that all women were like the one who cruelly mocked me ...

"Is ours also a lie? She asked, full of anxiety.

"No, Paule. Because if there is a universal truth, it is love. And when two creatures love each other, it is when they can affirm that they are rigorous and exact truth.

Horace Colton was close to the Frenchman who was guiding him, around Villesud, towards the German barracks. Sam Blue and eight more partisans followed.

The town was silent, with its quiet streets. A moon, in its last quarter, had risen just before the cloudiness of the clouds and cut out things to which it lent a ghostly appearance.

"It's there" said the Frenchman.

Horace looked at the house and saw the sentry, motionless, by the entrance. The rest of the barracks was in complete darkness.

"Are you sure the others have gone to Vichy?

"Yes. There is a party there and the Nazis will parade, along with the Laval militiamen.

"Sam and I," Horace said, "will take care of the sentry. You cover us. Understood?

"Yes.

"As soon as we have eliminated the German, we will go inside. Don't you think we could take some prisoners?

The truth is that he disgusted killing the defenseless.

"Bah! And what would we do with them?

"We could have them on the mountain, as hostages. Also, if there are any officers, they could provide us with reports for London.

"No" replied the other dryly. Comrade Marcel's orders are to kill these Nazi pigs.

"It's okay.

However, he did not quite understand too well that death wish that seemed to be the most important motive in the existence of the partisan group. The army had left too deep an imprint on his mind for him to be carried away by the savage violence of his new comrades.

He approached Sam and said in a low voice:

"You advance to the right. I'll do it on the left. Be very careful. The sentry is in a rather difficult place to surprise him.

"Agree.

Indeed, the barracks was located on one side of a kind of small square, with other buildings attached to it, which made it impossible to attack from behind the man who stood stiffly at the entrance.

Sam stepped forward, clutching the submachine gun in his sweaty hands.

Suddenly, when he had managed to get within twenty feet of the German, the latter saw him, immediately throwing his rifle at his face.

"Watch out, Sam! Horace yelled desperately.

Normally, Blue should have fired before his opponent, but he was ahead of him and Sam fell flat on his face, dropping the submachine gun. Colton then ran like a madman, receiving the second shot that, although it only went through his right arm, made him spin like a top, throwing him to one side as if a gigantic hand were hitting him all over the body.

One of the French threw a grenade.

With the sentry dead, the resisters rushed towards the gate, penetrating the barracks-house where the battle rapidly spread. Despite the fact that the first shots had awakened them, the sleeping Germans had no material time to organize their defense and were overwhelmed by the attackers' impetus.

Dozens of lights went on in the town.

Crawling, as he had been wounded again by the pieces of shrapnel from the grenade, thrown blindly by the French, Horace approached Blue's motionless body, realizing that he had died.

His chest ached extraordinarily, where perhaps some pieces of shrapnel had penetrated.

Pushing himself to his feet, he walked away from the barracks that the maquis were burning.

"I'm going to die?" " he asked himself.

An unspeakable anguish seized him. He had dreamed of coming home and he clung to that idea with all his might. It was completely impossible for anything serious to happen to him, "to him." Death could play with others, but he could not conceive that something similar could happen to him.

He was leaning on the walls of the houses.

As he approached the main square of the town, he heard a tremendous shouting, mixed with laments incomprehensible to him.

It didn't take long to find out.

When he came to a corner, where the street he had been walking on led to the square, he saw that it was profusely illuminated, and he shuddered as he watched the incredible spectacle unfolding before his incredulous eyes.

The square, like almost all those of all the towns of the world, was lined with trees, having in its center a monument to those killed in the First War, which had been destroyed by the Germans.

Cooper's voice rose above them all, shouting something Horace couldn't understand.

Eleven men hung from the branches of the trees and some resistant, with weapons in hand, stopped the wild impulse of women of all ages who shouted like crazy, trying to make their way into the square.

Some hanged men were still shuddering in the midst of the agonizing death throes.

Unable to contain himself any longer, Horace vomited in the corner, then backing away from there, eager to go back to the sergeant to tell him that the savage madness of the "Marcel" group hadn't stopped.

"Beasts! He murmured as he advanced, leaning on the cold walls of the houses.

The appearance of the group of assailants from the barracks, dragging the body of the dead officer inside the house, caused men and women to re-experience that chill of horror that had shaken them when they saw their men and friends hanging.

One of the maquis approached the «Tordu», who was laughing like a madman, pushing the feet of a hanged man with the tip of his rifle.

"Horace has disappeared" he told her.

The hunchback turned to him.

"English?

"Yes.

Santais was next to Cooper.

"Hey, comrade! Exclaimed the «Tordu».

"What's up?

"This one says that Horace has disappeared.

Santais's eyes flared with rage.

"Missing?

"Yes.

"Count, asshole!

"Blue was killed by the door. It was the sentry, who also wounded the other Englishman.

"And that?

"Leaving the barracks, I looked for both of them, but found only Sam... dead.

"How about?

"Bad. If that idiot saw about the plaza, he must have run to warn the sergeant. Was he very hurt?

"I do not know. The man replied.

"We have to do something! "Put in the hunchback.

"Of course" said Marcel. Grab a couple of men and head for the mountain. Try to get ahead of that English dog and when you see him, you fill his head with lead.

" It's okay! Hey, you two! Go!

"When this horrible war is over," said Adams, "I will take you to England. And once we get a divorce, we will get married and go away ...

"It will be very beautiful", she replied. You realize? A place where we can live without breathing this hatred that poisons the air of Europe.

"Yes. There are places on Earth where it is still possible to escape the stale air of this continent. Places where it is possible to feel alone, without the oppressive presence of a crowd that crawls, crawling incessantly, in something that they believe to be life.

You cannot imagine how far I have come to hate big cities. I have always lived in them, moving like a tiny piece in a gigantic machine, with hardly time to realize my own existence. Now, here, despite everything, how different things seem!

"It's as if from these heights we dominate the world and see it far away, strange, as if it had nothing to do with us.

And that's what happens, Adams. We have become different, different and apart from others.

Shaw rose to his feet, looking toward the grotto.

"I think they are calling," he said.

He had set the station ready for the reception that came to them every night from London.

Left alone, Paule stretched gluttonously. It gave him immense pleasure to feel her body, something he had come to sincerely hate, despising it as if it were a hideous curse that he had been forced to wear.

How could Adams's hands, his soft and powerful hands, have performed this wonderful transmutation?

"It is as if I had purified myself," she said to herself, moved, as if I were one of those men, of whom I have read so much, whose hands erase sin and clean everything ... "

She felt so deeply renewed that it was like a rebirth to life in which the past was gone, like something annoying, forever.

She stroked her hair and then her hands lowered, contouring her breasts to stop, trembling, on her smooth belly.

He closed his eyes, throwing his head back, eagerly breathing in the scented night air.

She had never been so deeply moved and now her hands were trying to caress her warmest chimera.

"Paule!

Horace's leaning, diminished silhouette was silhouetted against the starry background. There was something about the man that seemed to have changed his usual appearance. And seeing that he swayed, as if he had been drunk, she rushed towards him, grabbing him hard as he seemed to collapse.

Paule felt the hot, sticky liquid.

"Adams! She screamed, scared.

Shaw left the grotto and ran toward them. She scooped Horace into her arms and carried him to the entrance of the cave, laying him carefully on the blankets that Paule had hastily placed on the ground.

"Horace! My friend! Do not worry! We will heal you right away ...

Colton opened his eyes.

"It's useless, sir ...

"What nonsense are you saying?

"Listen ... they have hanged many in the square ... of Villesud. It's horrible ... they look like beasts ...

"You scoundrels!

"They... followed me... be careful... sir...

"Do not worry. We are going to heal you ... Paule!

She approached, trembling. It was then that a strange intuition made Horace turn his head into the dead of night.

"Watch out, sir! He yelled hoarsely.

The shot surprised Adams, who, moved by a reflex, hit the ground. Then Paule's cry of pain made him shudder from head to toe.

He got up, forgetting everything, running towards the girl who had fallen on her face.

"Paule!

He turned her around, taking her in his arms. Her eyes were wide open and a little red trickled out of her lips at one corner.

Some kind of flash exploded in Adams's head. Running to the grotto, crouching, he seized the submachine gun and left, just as the Tordu and the other two approached, weapons at the ready.

He had never pulled the trigger with such anger.

He kept shooting, even as the three men were lying on the ground and then he approached them, kicking the corpses.

"Dogs!" He groaned. You have killed her!

He dropped the submachine gun and returned to Paule. Then, remembering Horace, she moved closer to him, seeing that his body had definitely stiffened.

He went back to the woman's side.

Sitting on the floor, he stroked the dead woman's hair, then placed his hands on her belly.

How could I know?

Perhaps the stars, deep in space, knew the truth: that truth that she had sensed, as if something awakened deep within her.

" « Three Roses »calling ...

Here, 'Trafalgar Square'. Speak, «Three Roses» ...

"Suppress shipments immediately. The group works on its own, murdering civilians and not caring about anything else.

"Understand. Is it impossible to change the situation?

"Impossible. I intend to destroy the station and blow up all the ammunition and weapons that have been left in the camp.

"Good, Sergeant Shaw. We are very grateful to him for what he has done. Will you try to contact us later?

"I do not know. Now I'm going to cut ...

"Good luck!

"Thanks.

He pounded the station in rage. Then he went to the grotto where the weapons and ammunition were, preparing a charge of dynamite, the fuse of which he lit, then moving away to sit next to Paule's body.

The explosion shook the valleys, reproducing itself in a thousand different echoes.

"What could that have been? Marcel inquired.

The men were coming up the slope.

"I'm scared to think about it," Cooper said.

"The fact that?

"It must have blown everything up.

"Hey? Do you think he has gone crazy?

"The others should not have arrived on time. And Horace informed him, no doubt.

" Dog! Don't you know I'm going to tear you to pieces?

"You don't know him well, Marcel. You should never have trusted a Brit.

"And you?

"It is different.

"But, I can't believe I destroyed everything! He is convinced that Germany must be fought. What does it matter if we execute traitors? They are not English, after all ...

Cooper shrugged.

"I see you don't understand," Cooper said. Actually, it is difficult to understand. Only having lived with men like Adams can you understand certain things.

"Hang me if I understand you!

"Do not lose more time. We have to go up to see if we can save something ... although I would be surprised. Shaw will have done things as usual.

"Don't you know I'm going to hang up on you?

"Don't think about him ...

"Then?

"It's his way, Marcel. He is poisoned by a series of prejudices that are difficult to explain. He believes in the fight, but does not understand that it spreads to the point of dragging civilians. It's the old heritage of the English military ...

But have you not killed thousands of Indians?

"It's possible. Old Albion can afford certain things ... away from Europe. Here, you know how they do things. Don't you think it is ridiculous for the RAF to warn by radio so that the residents of a town to be bombed move away?

"Stupid!

"Stupid, but very British. "Playing fair" is called that ...

"Idiots! If that sergeant, or whatever, has destroyed our warehouse, I'll teach him our fair play! Go ahead!

He had buried Horace first and now he was finishing digging the grave for Paule.

When he drove the shovel into the pile of dirt he had scooped out, he approached the woman's body, kneeling beside her.

"I already told you, my dear" he whispered, feeling his eyes begin to sting ". It was impossible to escape. A great lie is around us and no one can escape its clutches ... I even think I lied to you when I told you that there were still places where you can live isolated from the world. There aren't any, Paule! Lies are like the atmosphere: they are everywhere.

And it is that nobody seems to have the right to live, to love, to feel sincerely human. If you want to do it, if you reach out to others, trying to show them that your heart is clean of hatred ... they are capable of severing your hands!

He took the body carefully.

Lifting it, he advanced slowly toward the pit. Then he knelt down again, bending over until he hurt himself to lay the corpse, as softly as possible, on the earthy, damp bottom of the hole.

His chest tore at the thought that all that wonderful body was going to be covered with earth soon after. The memories of the last days flooded his mind and he could no longer hold back the tears, which fell down his cheeks, bringing a bitter taste to his mouth, like bile feces ...

It was throwing the earth.

"Let's surround the camp" said Marcel. If you've done that, we can't let you get away.

"And Paule? Cooper asked.

"You like it, right? Santais said.

"Yes.

"I give it to you! And you can already be happy that I do not act with her in another way, after having failed in the mission that I entrusted to you.

The men dispersed, opening in a semicircle that gradually closed around the small plateau.

Advancing a little, Marcel screamed,

"Hey, Adams! We are here, comrade!

Putting the shovel on the ground, hearing Marcel's voice, Shaw sighed deeply. Then he went to the cave and picked up another submachine gun, since there were always two next to the station, which now lay shattered, showing a complicated network of cables emerging from its torn cover.

"Adams! Marcel called again.

The Briton put the weapon into working order and went out, straight, advancing into the darkness of the night, already beginning to pale in the East.

"Adams! We are here! You haven't destroyed anything, right?

"Horace lied to you! He was a fascist! You'll see the great things we're going to do together!

The light of dawn lazily advanced, staining the edges of the night's mantle with lilac.

"When I was little, I thought stars were holes ..."

"You sure haven't destroyed anything! I already told you that I was never wrong with men ... and you are a formidable guy!

It's only true when two love each other, darling. Because in doing so, the lie cannot penetrate them, which love makes impenetrable to evil ... »

"Speak up, Adams! What was that explosion that we heard? It was Horace! It is not true?

«I promise you that I have forgotten it, my love. There is no longer a first of May in my heart ... I swear! »

"We are watching you, Adams! But we will not shoot ... We will continue to work together!

The sergeant advanced a little further. Then it stopped.

And pulled the trigger.

END